*A*
*Harlequin*
*Romance*

OTHER
*Harlequin Romances*
by MARY WIBBERLEY

# DARK VIKING

by

## MARY WIBBERLEY

**HARLEQUIN BOOKS**   TORONTO
WINNIPEG

Original hard cover edition published in 1975
by Mills & Boon Limited.

© Mary Wibberley 1975

SBN 373-01879-7

Harlequin edition published May 1975

Printed in Canada

1879

# CHAPTER ONE

EMMA LAING looked resolutely at the shiny oilskin coat that lay over her knees. If she watched it hard, really concentrated on it, the other sensation might just go away ...

'It will not be long now, miss. Just a half hour or so.' The voice was meant to be reassuring, and she looked up and smiled faintly, then wished she hadn't. She knew that you couldn't actually die of seasickness—at least she had never heard of it happening, but there was always a first time ... And half an hour more.

'I must be mad.' She said the words out loud, but the wind whipped them away and the boatman never turned his head. Grey misty rain hung low like a cloud and gently touched her face before being blown away by the small playful gusts that only added to her general discomfort. Emma thought back with wistful longing to the warm cushioned comfort of the flight from London to Aberdeen, the only slightly less luxurious boat from there to Lerwick—and now this. This being a boat that had seemed faintly romantic-looking when she had first seen it. But no one had told her how rough the sea could be. She looked in faint alarm at the man steering the vessel as a huge wave lifted and then dropped them. There was nothing in the set of his shoulders to indicate alarm or fear. Wasn't he bothered? Didn't he realize the awful danger—and then she heard the faint whistling, the strains of 'Nut-Brown Maiden' before the wind took that too, and she leaned back, only slightly reassured. At least he wasn't bothered. Perhaps they would make it after all. Just at that moment Emma didn't really

5

care. Judith's words came back to her, from the previous morning.

'You won't regret it, love, honestly. I only wish I had the chance to come up with you, but with John coming home any time——' a shrug, Judith's calm face lit by the spark of love that came whenever she spoke about her husband. 'But it will do you good, a break like that, and to get away from that brute Robert. I'm only surprised you've never gone up there before. If I'd had a house left me, I'd have been up like a shot, if only out of curiosity, instead of leaving it for two years.'

Two years. It had not seemed that long. The past two years had gone by so fast that Emma had scarcely had time to stop and take stock of herself, or think. Twenty-four whirlwind months during which her career had soared, she had met and become engaged to Robert, and life had seemed boundlessly perfect. Until two weeks previously, when she had broken off the engagement, and suddenly discovered that life as a top model was damned hard work and she had had enough of it, and of men, and of London—and everything.

'You're just depressed because of Robert, that's all it is. You need a holiday—so why not take one? You can afford it, and you've got the perfect place to go to.' Judith's words fell like a drop of common sense in Emma's private sea of turmoil and had sparked off the idea. And here she was. But she wasn't ready to think about Robert yet, except that it had been the biggest shock in the world to discover that Judith didn't like him, had never liked him, and was relieved that the engagement was over.

'There she lies, miss. Yonder.' Emma had really given up thoughts of ever actually touching dry land again and she looked in the direction of the pointing arm with a kind of abstract interest. It was real enough, the grey rocky land

6

mass, the long thin strip of shingle, green springy wind-blown grass stretching away for ever.

'This is it? Skeila?' Her heart sank. Was it too late to turn back? Yes, it was. The boat from Aberdeen had arrived in Lerwick at six that morning and Emma had breakfasted and then walked around. How right it had all seemed then, just strolling round drinking in the clean morning air, admiring the solid stone buildings, pink and grey and cream, seeing the waiting blue and white buses by the harbour, and the boats ... A perfect backdrop for those modelling assignments where you stood by the water in an elegant sweater and skirt, watched by an admiring fisherman or two, and the photos appeared in all the glossy magazines and made women reach for their phones, to call their nearest big store ... But that had been Lerwick. This was not. It was Skeila, and she owned a house on it and she had not imagined it would be quite so bleak.

'Oh no!' She didn't mean to say it aloud, but she had, because the boatman looked at her and grinned, and said:

'I'll put your cases down for you, miss.'

But I want to go back. Now. She looked at him, and the words were unspoken, but they were in her eyes in a kind of desperate appeal, and something must have reached him, for he shook his head slowly.

'The weather is a little sad at the moment, but it will change—you see.'

He was helping her out now, her last link with the civilized world, about to abandon her. She scrambled over the side, feeling her shoes sink into damp shingle, still slightly queasy, although this was terra firma, or nearly.

'I—I don't know where my house is,' she said, wondering if she looked as dreadful as she felt. There was a cluster of grey stone houses in the distance, a bright red phone box near the first. And nothing else. No one moving, not even an animal nor a bird.

'Anyone will tell you. Will I carry your cases to the nearest house now?'

'Yes, please.' She had paid him before they had left Lerwick. She didn't know if he was in a hurry to get away, but she wanted to make sure that at least someone else was alive on this barren place before she let him depart. His ruddy weatherlined face was assuming more the aspect of a guardian angel with every second that passed. 'If you wouldn't mind,' she added.

'Ach, it is no trouble at all.' His accent was pleasant and musical in tone, certainly not a typical Scots one to her unaccustomed ear.

He walked at an easy pace along the track towards the houses. Emma could see a street now, and that one of the houses was a shop with a window full of goods and a sign above that announced its owner to be: 'J. Grant. General Provision Merchant.' The board was blue and white, and faded by the weather, and she wondered when it had last been painted.

Several small craft were beached, and two more bobbed in the water, and a fat white gull sat on one and watched them with beady yellow eyes. Emma looked up at the heavy grey clouds sweeping past, and shivered. Could it be that she was still asleep on the boat, and this was all a bad dream?

'Eh, you'll not have been up here before?' They were nearly there at the first house now, and it was no dream, because cold fine rain suddenly began to fall and it was too real to be imagined. Emma pulled up the collar of her short grey furry jacket and shook her head.

'No. This is the first time. I have a house here—somewhere.' The last word seemed to echo round them in lost fashion, and the man nodded.

8

'Ah! And you're here for a wee holiday?'

'Yes.' She had planned on two weeks, but—'Are you on the phone?' she asked desperately.

'Aye. I'll write my number on a piece of paper for you.'

He put down her two smart blue cases and rapped on the bright red door of the first house. A geranium stood on the windowsill, and the flower nodded in brave competition with the door, and the lace curtains twitched a fraction, then a voice called:

'Ah, it's Dougall. Come away in.'

'I have a young woman here,' he bellowed, then added to Emma, unnecessarily: 'They're deaf. You'll have to speak up.'

'Yes, I see.' And that's all I need, she thought, then chided herself for cruelty.

The door opened. A very old woman stood there. Dressed entirely in black, she looked up at them and gave them both a broad toothless smile.

'Come in. I have the kettle on just now.'

Dougall looked doubtfully at Emma. 'She will be hurt if you don't,' he said quietly, and Emma smiled.

'Of course.' The smell of food came from the interior—and to her surprise she discovered that not only had the sick feeling gone, but she was desperately hungry.

The room was stiflingly warm with a huge fire roaring up the chimney, and a great cat sitting on the rug in front of it. It took her eyes a few seconds to adjust to the gloom. The furniture was old and huge, a long hard settee nearly filling one side, old prints of racehorses on the walls, a wind-up gramophone in one corner and an aspidistra lording it over the row of geraniums on the table.

'Sit you down. You'll both have tea?'

The smell was quite clear now. Somewhere in an oven a steak and kidney pie was just about ready to be eaten.

9

Emma wondered if she would faint from hunger before she had finished her cup of tea. To keep her slender model's figure she existed almost solely on salads and grilled fish and eggs, and had not eaten a steak and kidney pie for years, but now, suddenly, it was the one thing she craved above everything else.

'I'm sorry?' She looked up, startled out of her daydream as she realized the old woman was speaking to her.

'Maybe you would care for a wee bite to eat?' Perhaps because of her deafness, the old lady shouted, but the words were so welcome that Emma could have kissed her.

'Oh—if it's no trouble——' she remembered just in time to speak up. 'Yes, please.'

'Aye, well, there's a pie in the oven. You'll be very welcome. My sister is about to serve it now. You'll have some, Dougall?'

Dougall nodded, waited until the old woman had gone out to the kitchen, presumably to check up and report the change of events to her sister, and spoke to Emma.

'This will make their day, having a visitor,' he told her. 'You'll not mind staying a while?'

If only he knew! 'No,' Emma answered. 'I'm not in a hurry.'

'Ah, that's all right, then. And they can tell you exactly where your house is afterwards. I dare say they'll take you.'

'What are their names?' she asked.

'Janet and Margaret Murray——' and she heard the first old lady's voice from the kitchen:

'Young Dougall has brought us a visitor, Margaret. A girl.' So the one who had opened the door was Janet—and Emma's guide was *young* Dougall. Emma looked at him to see if he was smiling at this description, but he appeared not to have noticed.

Margaret was like her sister, so much so that they could

10

have been twins. And they could cook, no doubt about it. Emma had to restrain herself from falling on the full plate of steaming pie surrounded by carrots and potatoes. She gave a fleeting thought to her diet, shrugged and got on with it.

Dougall stayed for a while, then got up, wrote his phone number on the back of a crumpled envelope and handed it to Emma with the words:

'You'll let me know when you want me,' and smiled. There was something about that smile that puzzled her. It was as if he knew something she didn't.

It was clear that the two old ladies were bursting with curiosity, equally obvious that natural good manners were fighting a losing battle with their desire to know who she was and why she was there. Emma, over a mug of hot tea, told them. Dougall had departed, the cat still slept, and outside the wind whipped the rain against the windows in a muted rat-a-tat that made the room seem so much warmer and snug. And Emma began her story, quite unaware, in her concentration to make sure that they could hear every word, of the startled reaction those words were receiving.

'I have a house here, but I don't know exactly where it is,' she said slowly and loudly. 'A great-uncle died over two years ago and left it to me.' She paused to let the two old women look at one another and nod.

'Eh—that would be Edward Laing, then?'

'Yes!' Relief filled Emma. 'You know where it is? My name is Emma Laing.' As one of London's top models, her name was usually guaranteed to cause instant reaction from anyone to whom it was mentioned, a sort of double-take, and: '*The* Emma Laing!' Nothing like that here. She smiled to herself. Clearly her only claim to attention was the fact that she now owned Edward Laing's house.

'Aye, we know,' Janet answered, and nodded. 'But no

one has been near it for two years.'

'Yes. I've been meaning to come up, but I was very busy——' she paused, something of her usual self-possession deserting her at their expressions. Were they *worried* about something?

'Young Greg won't be very pleased,' Janet commented in a loud aside to her sister. Margaret pursed her lips, and Emma began to get the strangest feeling that they had forgotten she was there.

'Indeed and he will not. Oh dear!'

And who was young Greg? Emma decided to find out. 'Young Greg?' she said with a bright smile.

'Aye. Greg Halcro. He doesn't like being bothered.' Janet looked sadly at Emma. 'The birds, you know.'

'The birds,' Emma repeated. She didn't feel capable of saying anything else. 'But where is young Greg?' It was like a title, and remembering their description of Dougall, who was fifty if he was a day, it seemed possible that young Greg was some elderly crofter—but a bird fancier? Emma put her hand to her head. No, it was quite cool, she had no temperature.

'Why, it's the next cottage he has to your uncle's—to yours.'

'Oh, I see.' Her heart sank. Things had seemed to improve when she had first smelt that delicious pie. They seemed to be going rapidly awry again. 'And doesn't he like strangers?' She should never have come. She had known it on the boat. Oh, why had she let Dougall go?

'No.' Janet's face softened, seeing Emma's dismay. 'Ach, his bark is worse than his bite, I'm sure. It's just—well——' and she bit her lip.

'What?' Emma clutched her bag.

'Well, he was very annoyed about the house being left so long——'

12

Oh, he was, was he? Emma's flagging spirits jolted to a halt. He was one of those nosey-parker old men who minded other people's business instead of his own. So *that* was it! She looked up, and there was a new light in her sherry brown eyes as she looked from one sister to the other, and smiled. This was nothing to do with them, they were being kindness itself, but if they thought some man was going to prevent her from going to her own cottage ...

'Thank you for telling me,' she said. 'I'll have to see him and explain, won't I?' And tell him to mind his own affairs, she added to herself. One thing that five years of modelling had taught her was the ability to look after herself, not to be pushed around by anyone.

'Well,' Janet looked at her sister. 'We'd best take Miss Laing there now, what do you think?'

'Oh, but——' Emma protested. 'You've been so kind, I can't let you go out in this. If you'll just describe how I——'

'Nonsense!' Janet looked towards the window. 'It's a wee bit of rain, that's all. A fine day for a walk.'

A wee bit of rain! Emma smiled faintly. In London she would have taken a taxi, but here there was none. 'You're very kind——' she began.

'Ach, it's a pleasure to have someone here. Just sit a while and drink your tea. There's no hurry. No hurry at all.'

The rain stung at her face, legs and bare hands as she struggled along the narrow road. Emma refused to look at her shoes at all, and sighed for the elegant boots packed in one case. They would at least have been a bit warmer. Janet and Margaret strode along at her side. She had had a battle to stop them carrying her luggage for her. Clad in ancient mackintoshes and wellingtons, they were quite clearly enjoying their walk. Janet carried the small shopping bag full of groceries that Emma had bought at the general store before setting out. And in Emma's mind was a vision of the pot of tea she was going to make for them all before they set off on the return journey home. She knew that the house had been left fully furnished, and the first job, after lighting a good fire, was to air the bedding she would need ... Her mind raced ahead, planning, resolutely not thinking about 'young Greg'. She would take care of him afterwards. When the old ladies had departed.

There was the distant sound of an engine, growing nearer, and Emma looked around quickly. A Land-Rover was belting along at a fair speed from the direction of the houses they had so recently left behind. Emma called out: 'There's a car coming,' because it didn't look as if it intended stopping for anything or anyone—and they would not hear it.

They stopped, looked round, then at each other, and Janet pulled a face. 'Aye, it's him.' She raised her stick and waved it, and the Land-Rover screeched to a halt only feet away. And Emma looked, because she had a horrible feeling ...

And then the man got out and walked over to them, and her heart lurched in a most odd way. *This* was young Greg? She swallowed hard. Here was no elderly birdwatcher. He was a giant of a man, easily six feet four, dressed in thick Shetland sweater, black trousers tucked into wellingtons—but it was his face that she found herself watching, quite unable to help herself. She had met all kinds of males in the short course of her modelling career. She had learned to tell the sheep from the wolves, the mice from the men ... but she had never seen one like this before.

He was all man. Hard tanned face, a jutting chin, wide

14

mouth, straight nose—and grey eyes that were as hard as that face. Thick dark hair looked as if a combing would not come amiss, and he ran his fingers through it now, almost as if he read Emma's thoughts, though he spared her not a glance. He looked straight at Margaret and Janet and just for a second she glimpsed something behind the hardness. Then he smiled.

'Good day, ladies. Can I give you a lift somewhere?' He had a deep voice, an intriguing accent, and the two old women looked at each other and smiled, then at him again.

'Well, we were coming in your direction——' Emma listened, amazed. No doubt about it, there was a girlish flutter in that voice. She gave him a very casual sidelong glance. He stood there, all six feet four of him, towering easily over the three of them, and just at that moment, as he listened to Janet's explanation of where they were going, and why, he looked directly at Emma, and she received the full force of an electrifying gaze. It was a distinct shock—but the words that followed were even more so.

'So you're coming to Craig House at last?' Inoffensive enough themselves, but not the way he said them, the subtle emphasis on the last two. Emma's hackles rose. Now she knew precisely what the two dear old ladies had been trying to tell her.

'Yes, I am.' She was not going to indulge in a duel of words with him. Not here, not yet. So she smiled, and saw his mouth tighten, noticed the muscles tense in his jaw, and experienced a tiny stab of satisfaction. She had come here to get away from men, had come for peace and quiet, the chance to sort out a lot of things in her mind. And if this tough-looking character thought he was going to tell her what she could and could not do, he was in for a big surprise.

'Right. Then we'd better get in the Land-Rover.' He

turned to Janet. 'I think you and Miss Murray can squeeze in the front seat. Miss Laing will go in the back——' and he spared her a brief glance that encompassed her now muddy shoes and spattered tights. He looked away again before his expression changed, but Emma thought she saw it—an amused contempt.

'Oh, but——' Janet was protesting. 'We only came to show Miss Laing the *way*, you see. If you're going——' her voice tailed away, almost wistfully. They had probably been looking forward to a little visit. Emma experienced a moment of panic. They couldn't leave her alone—with *him!*

'I'm sure Miss Laing would be glad of your help in settling in,' he said slowly and clearly, so that they could hear every word. And Emma gave a little sigh. A showdown there might have to be—but she was not prepared for it yet.

'Maybe, Miss Laing, it would be better if you got in first. Then I'll pass you your cases. You might care to sit on one. I'm afraid the back of my Land-Rover isn't built for passengers.'

She saw what he meant as she scrambled in. Ropes and fishing rods and assorted boxes lay in the back, in no sort of order, and the interior smelt of petrol and fish and tweed. Emma gritted her teeth. He hadn't done it deliberately, because he hadn't known, and certainly wouldn't expect the two old women to sit there, but she sensed the covert amusement in his eyes as he assisted the two in. She was beginning to experience a feeling of intense dislike for this dark stranger—and one thing was quite certain—the feeling was mutual.

'Right. Hold tight.' The words might have been addressed to her or they might not. The way he drove, they were needed. It could have been the road, or the springs,

16

but she had never been so uncomfortable in her life. The last stage of her journey—and undoubtedly the worst. London, and comfort, seemed a million light miles away as she hung on grimly to the framework inside the back of the dark vehicle. She glared at the back of his head as he drove swiftly along. A hair-cut wouldn't do him any harm either, she thought. Perhaps he just used garden shears occasionally.

And how far was Craig House? She could see nothing from where she sat, only a thin ribbon of road ahead, nearly obscured by driving rain. A wave of unhappiness engulfed Emma. What on earth was she doing here? Oh, if only Judith had been able to come! How different when there was someone to talk to, someone on your own wavelength, to laugh off all the mishaps, to share the fun. And then something that had been said came back to her. Greg was her *neighbour*. That meant ... But she forgot exactly what it meant as the vehicle swerved and bumped upwards, up a rough track, and she knew without being told that this was it. They would be here any minute now—and then she would see her house for the first time ever. The rocking, swaying motion stopped. They were still. Greg turned to look at her. Then he climbed out and walked round the front to open the passenger door. He leaned in after helping the sisters out and his hard grey eyes held no expression at all as he asked: 'Can you manage?'

'Yes, thank you.' And damn you, she added mentally. Emma was agile and adept at scrambling out of awkward places, an ability for which she was grateful at that moment, because she moved lithely forward and jumped down to the ground. She was aware of him reaching inside the vehicle for her cases, but she was too busy looking towards the row of cottages before her. The two old ladies were watching her and she tried to hide the dismay that she felt

17

at this, the first sight of her legacy. Three in a row, but one of them a tumbledown ruin, and she didn't need to guess which was hers, for the furthest one had smoke curling from the chimney, and bright red curtains at the windows. It was the middle one, forlorn and cold-looking, thick grey stone and grey roof and a door that had once been green, or maybe brown, but was now an obscure matt dullness, that gave no welcome. None at all.

'There it is. You have a key, of course, Miss Laing?'

'Of course.' She looked at him as he stood there with her cases. It would not have surprised her at all if he had handed them to her, but he didn't, just moved off carrying them to that bleak door, followed by the two old ladies. After a moment's hesitation Emma went too. Rain fell, steady and relentless, neither cold nor warm, just very wet. She had not felt so miserable for a while.

The sea was there, just the other side of the track, the shore hidden by cliffs, but even so there came the muted roar, and she knew there would be rocks below. She fumbled in her bag for the key that the solicitor in Lerwick had sent her a few days previously. She should have gone to Cornwall, where some friends had a bungalow, and a permanent open invitation—but she had listened to Judith instead. And now she was here.

They were waiting for her by the door, the three of them, the two old ladies with kindly faces and that one big man whose hostile eyes told her only too clearly that she was not wanted. Emma pushed the key in the lock and tried to turn it. Nothing happened. The deep voice came softly:

'Let me try.' It was not her imagination. She *knew* he was enjoying her discomfiture, knew it as surely as if he had said it. She moved her hand away quickly and he reached out and tried to turn the key, and stopped.

18

'It's jammed,' he said. 'Probably with not being used for so long.'

Nothing in the words, just in the way he said them, and her mouth tightened helplessly. Oh God, I hate him, she thought.

'I'll tell you what,' he went on, looking at the two mackintoshed old women. 'You'll all get soaked standing here. We'll go into my house and I'll then come back and try and open it.'

There was no warning when he opened his front door and the two huge alsatians bounded out. Emma froze momentarily, the two sisters trotted in quite unconcerned, and Greg Halcro looked at her. 'They won't hurt you,' he remarked. 'Down, Bess, Meg.'

She looked at them, then at him. If this was a test she was determined not to fail it. 'I like dogs,' she said, and put out her hand for them to sniff. Then she smiled at the watching man and walked into the room that led directly off from the front door.

A fire burned brightly, and an opened newspaper lay over the back of the settee in front of it. The dark red carpet seemed to have a warmth of its own as well, and the atmosphere of the room was one of comfort and welcome.

Greg moved the paper. 'I'll get the kettle on,' he told them. 'Do sit down.' He vanished into the kitchen and Emma heard a tap running, the sound of metal against metal, the plop and hiss as gas was lit. She did not want to sit down, but she had no choice. Bess and Meg were lying in front of the two old women who had made themselves comfortable on the settee. Emma sat in a hard-backed chair by the window and observed the room. There was a television in one corner, and beside it a stereogram. Her fingers itched to riffle through the dozens of records beside it and she looked quickly away. She didn't want to know what his

19

taste was.

She didn't care—and in any case she was only here on sufferance, because her door wouldn't open, and two old women could not be left standing in the rain. She had a sudden desire to see his kitchen, and knew that she probably wouldn't get another chance. Before she had time to analyse her reasons she stood and went into it.

'Can I help you, Mr. Halcro?' she asked sweetly. He looked round.

'I can manage, thanks,' he answered. 'As soon as I've made this I'll go and get your door open.' His presence filled the room with power. The antagonism—undeclared yet mutual—was a tangible force between them. He had not switched on a light in the kitchen and the room was shadowy and dark, and Emma felt suddenly frightened of him. She moved slightly away as he turned towards her, but he was only going into a cupboard. He reached in and shook a tin. 'Biscuits,' he said, and he was smiling because he had seen her flinch, and she was annoyed with herself. The cold prickles of dislike touched her skin and she felt cold.

'Then I'll go back,' she said.

'I should. And take these in—please,' he added softly. 'I'll not be a minute, then I'll open your door for you.' He handed her the biscuit tin.

A few minutes later, as she sat again by the window in her hard chair, half listening to the two old ladies fussing the dogs, breaking off pieces of shortbread for them, she watched Greg Halcro walk out of the front door, heard it close behind him, and waited for him to return and tell her that she could go into her house.

Minutes passed, and he walked in and handed her the key, still warm from his touch. 'The door's unlocked,' he said. 'It's all yours.' The grey eyes seemed to mock her, but she met their challenge with her own.

'Thanks. You're very kind.'

'It's very cold in there—doubtless damp after all this time. Not really fit to stay in. Are you *sure* you know what you're doing?'

Emma stood up. He wasn't even being subtle about it now. She faced him, only her heightened breathing betraying her feelings. She knew that the two old women, happily engrossed with the animals, could not hear her.

'You don't get rid of me quite so easily, Mr. Halcro,' she said forcefully. 'Though I'm sure you're doing your best. Why, I don't know. But I'll tell you one thing. You can be abominably rude with very little effort!'

One dark eyebrow lifted slightly. 'The girl's got spirit,' he commented. 'Well, well!' He shook his head. 'But if I were you I'd watch that sharp tongue. It won't do you any good with me—and if you tell me to go to hell you can hardly come in begging for coal five minutes later, now can you?'

Emma took a deep breath. Coal! What if there were none? What if she did—but it was too awful to contemplate. She looked at him. He was an utter beast. She had met him for the first time only half an hour previously, hardly time to form the barest impression of anyone. Yet of one thing she was now quite sure. She had never in all her life met anyone she disliked as much as Greg Halcro.

# CHAPTER TWO

THERE was worse to come. Less than fifteen minutes later the four of them were standing in the living room of Emma's house, and she looked around her, heart sinking rapidly as she saw her inheritance properly for the first time. In a way it might not have been so bad if she hadn't just come out of Greg Halcro's warm comfortable house. The contrast was so much starker. And the awful thing was—he knew it.

The two old ladies didn't. They were busy looking round, exclaiming at how quickly it could all be made habitable with a good fire and a wee bit of polish, and some nice curtains at the windows ... But Emma barely heard them. If only Judith were here now, to share her feelings. They might even find humour in the situation, as they usually did. She watched Greg Halcro cross to the fire and crouch down. She heard his shocked, indrawn breath, and waited. What now?

'The chimney looks as if it needs sweeping to me,' he said, looking round. 'The room will be full of smoke if you're not careful.'

Emma wondered what the two old ladies would do if she gave way to temptation and went over and hit him *hard*. He was revelling in the situation, taking an almost sadistic satisfaction at finding all the faults he possibly could.

'I'll chance it,' she answered. There was soot in the hearth; it had been there quite a time from the look of it. 'I'll go out to the back and see if there's any fuel.'

He stood up, wiping his hands on the seat of his trousers.

'I can save you the trouble. There is some—but not a lot. You'll have to be economical if you want it to last, while you're here.'

'Oh, I see. Thank you.' She gave him a smile, because for some reason he didn't like them. Perhaps, she thought, he'd prefer to see me crying. 'Maybe there's an electric fire?' She regretted the question instantly as he shook his head.

'It wouldn't be much use if there were,' he said gently. 'No electricity.'

'But you——' her eyes widened. 'You've got television!' It was an absurd thing to say, but it was all she could think of.

'Ah yes, but I have electricity, you see.' He spoke as if to a backward child. 'Powered by a kind of windmill thing in the back garden. You'll see it if you look out from your kitchen window,' he added helpfully.

She walked out of the living room into the kitchen. Not to see his 'windmill thing' but because she wondered how she was going to cook. He followed her out, saw her staring at the gas stove, her expression of relief at the sight of it, and said in that cool dark voice that she was beginning to loathe: 'Calor gas. Keep your fingers crossed that there's some in the tank.'

He went over and crouched down at the cylinder beside the old-fashioned cooker and turned on a tap. Then he stood and switched on a jet. Gas hissed. He turned it off. 'You're lucky,' he remarked. 'It seems okay.'

She couldn't resist the retort. 'And aren't you sorry!'

He looked at her. 'I don't know what you mean,' but the merest glimmer of a quirk at his mouth betrayed the lie.

'You damn well do. If I turned and walked out now, you'd be delighted!' She hadn't meant this to happen, but the tension was unbearable, and she couldn't help herself.

'So let me tell you something, Mr. Halcro. You don't get rid of me so easily.'

He looked shocked. 'Get rid? Rather dramatic words, Miss Laing. You must be tired after your long journey. From London, is it? No doubt you'll feel better after a good meal and a rest.'

'I've had a good meal, thank you, and I'm not tired. All I want to do is settle down in my house and get a fire lit. I'm—I'm looking forward to my holiday here, as a matter of fact,' and at that moment she believed her own words.

'Oh, I'm sure you are. There's not much to do here of course, but then it will be a change for you after your job—after all, it can't be much fun working in the big city, can it?'

'It all depends what you do there. *My* job is very interesting and satisfying.' It was ridiculous, having the feeling that she needed to justify herself to this extremely aggressive, rude man.

'Hm,' he nodded, as though in polite agreement. 'But of course you needed to get away from it, so you remembered your little house. Very handy.'

'Yes, wasn't it?' she agreed sweetly. She would *not* let him get the better of her, damn him! 'And you live here all the time. Tell me, Mr. Halcro, do you ever go away for a holiday?' and she smiled at him.

'Occasionally.'

'It would be more for a change of air, I imagine—I mean, after all, as you said, there's not much to do here, is there? Not for an active-looking man such as yourself.'

He laughed. 'Ah, I see. What you're wondering, of course, is whether I actually work'—she was annoyed to find herself going pink at his blunt interpretation of her words—'oh, yes, I have plenty to keep me busy, Miss Laing, don't concern yourself with that. I don't laze about,

24

I assure you.'

She widened her eyes. 'Heavens, did I say you did?'

'No, but the implication was there. I'm writing a book about the birds on these islands—there are many varieties, as you will doubtless discover on your walks. And while we're on the subject, I would advise you always to take a walking stick with you when—if—you do go out.'

'Why?' Despite everything else, she was intrigued by something in his words.

'Because the arctic tern and the skua—two of the birds which abound—make swooping attacks on people walking. An upraised stick will deflect their swoops. You have to be quite careful if you venture into their areas.' The disbelief on Emma's face must have been obvious, for he added: 'You don't have to accept what I say—you'll certainly find out for yourself.'

'Thanks for telling me. I shall store the advice away. I intend to go for lots of long walks while I'm here.'

'Then I hope you have good walking shoes.' She paused on her way to unlock the back door. Damn him!

'I have, thanks.' She reached up to undo the top bolt. It wouldn't move. She gritted her teeth and jerked as hard as she could, but the bolt seemed to resist even more strongly than before.

'Allow me.' He had waited until she had nearly torn her fingernails. A hand came over hers and she moved quickly away, suddenly disturbed by his nearness. Emma was very tall, nearly five feet nine, but she felt absurdly small next to this man—and oddly defenceless. She watched as he eased the bolt free—no effort needed with him. He turned round and grinned at her.

'Gently does it.' He bent and pulled back the bottom bolt. 'That's it. You'd better oil those—if you have any oil, that is. You don't want to be struggling every night and morning, do you?'

'I had heard that people didn't need to bolt their doors in these parts because everyone was honest,' she answered quickly.

'True—usually,' and he appeared to hesitate, then shrugged. 'But I would advise it.'

Her breath quicked. Was this just another attempt to frighten her away? He'd been doing a pretty good job so far—and yet there was that certain something in his words that caused her a pang of disquiet.

'Tell me what you mean,' she said quickly. He looked straight into her eyes. Grey, dark, disturbing, his own were not mocking—not at that moment.

'I mean there are strangers about these islands. Just take my advice.'

'You're trying to scare me,' she jerked out, but a pulse beat in her throat and betrayed her.

'No. This is a remote spot—surely you've noticed that? And I sleep like a log once I'm in bed.' For the first time since meeting him, Emma had the feeling that he was quite serious—even sincere. She felt a prickle run up her spine, and turned quickly away before he could see how his words had affected her.

'I'll take your advice,' she said. 'I'll go and see if the old ladies want a cup of tea.'

'Then I'll get your cases. Excuse me.' He opened the back door and went out. Emma watched him go. Her feelings were very mixed. Just then, for a minute, the dislike had vanished and she had glimpsed another aspect of the man's personality. What it was she did not know. She turned away and went into the living room.

The fire was lit. Emma was alone. Greg Halcro had run the two Misses Murray back home after they had stayed for another cup of tea. It was very quiet now, a strange contrast to what had been before.

She put the blankets, spread carefully over two chairs, nearer the fire, and looked at the orange depths and cheerful yellow crackling flames. She was filthy after all her efforts and longed for nothing so much as a long soak in a hot bath. But there was more work to be done first. Sheets and pillowcases to be found upstairs, the rooms to be dusted, the sweeper run over the carpets, and then with a little luck the water would be hot enough. Emma bent and peered hopefully up the chimney to check that the handle was open to allow the fire to draw. She loved to see an open fire but longed for the simplicity of an electric one.

Uppermost in her mind was the thought of the conversation she intended to have with Judith. After a bath and some tea she was going to walk back to the village and telephone her from the box. Emma's mouth curved in a little smile at the thought. 'Oh, have I got some things to tell you,' she said, speaking out loud. 'Just you wait!'

There was a fireguard which she put in front of the flames while she went to dust and clean the carpets. It was hard work, but strangely satisfying to see the house gradually take on a more cheerful aspect as it became cleaner. The fire burned well and she had polished the stone hearth with some special cleaner she had found. Emma stood back to survey her work when at last it was completed, and gave a deep sigh of satisfaction. Now for a bath.

She saw her face in the bathroom mirror, and after the first shock, began to laugh. Dirt smudged, her hair escaping from its scarf—none of her friends would have recognized her, that was certain.

She sank into the warm water, glad that she had thought to pack her bath oil. She wondered briefly if Greg Halcro had returned. She hadn't heard the Land-Rover, but she had been too busy anyway. As the grime soaked away, together with all the aches and twinges from unaccustomed hard work, Emma allowed her thoughts to go to the dark hostile man who had made it quite clear that she was not welcome. But why? Surely not simply because he was writing a book about birds? What could she do to stop that? It was more, much more, she sensed. In a way it was almost frightening. She didn't want to admit it to herself, but she knew why.

He was a hard powerful man—but more; she had observed him when he had been busy doing something just before the old ladies went. He had been trying to release the window catches in the kitchen, and had been unaware and unconcerned with Emma's scrutiny. There was a ruthless determination about his face as he worked. He was a man who got what he wanted. He wanted Emma to go away. Would he succeed? She had almost forgotten her own reluctance to stay when she had first arrived in the face of his hostile opposition. It was a challenge, something she had not faced for a while, certainly not in her job. It was stimulating; she had no intention of meekly acquiescing to anything he wanted. He had no right or reason to be so downright aggressive. Emma sank back in the bath and her beautiful eyes lit with the light of battle. 'Right, Mr. Young Greg Halcro,' she said softly to a fly on the ceiling, 'let's see how we get on, shall we?' And in a strange way she began to look forward to their next encounter. And of the man called Robert, her so recent fiancé, she thought not at all.

'What ? Emma? It's really you—oh, Emma!' Judith's voice came over the line as clearly as if she were just next door, and Emma, who was so full of her own news, didn't hear the suppressed excitement in her friend's voice.

'Judith, honestly, if you knew—hang on, let me put in a ten-pence piece—oh, damn those pips—are you there? Good. Listen, love, I've arrived safely, and got the house cleaned up, but I was cursing you when I arrived! And there's this *awful* man who wants to get rid of me——'

'What? What do you mean?' Judith's voice cut in, worriedly.

Emma laughed. 'Oh, he's not trying to bump me off or anything—not yet anyway—but he's doing his damnedest to put me off staying here. He's a bird-watcher or something equally odd——'

'What's he like? Old?'

'Old?' Emma smiled. 'Heavens, no. About thirty-five, I think, a big hulking brute——'

'Cor! What's he look like?'

'Um, dark—not bad looking really, if you like that sort of thing.' Emma could see his face quite clearly, which was odd, considering everything. 'Very big, and broad-shouldered, and he's got two giant alsatians which scared the life out of me. He lives next door'—Judith snorted with laughter—'and he drives a scruffy Land-Rover and calls me Miss Laing with ice in his voice and keeps implying that I'll never survive and why don't I go, and——'

'John can't come home for another month,' Judith interrupted her.

'What?' Emma clutched the phone, and then as the pips went again, stuck in another coin quickly. 'Oh, what's the matter, Judith?'

'Nothing!' Judith's laugh floated over the miles. 'Only the installation of some new top-secret machinery has been held up, so they want him to stay in Ottawa until they can get them done. Don't you see? I could have come up with you.'

Emma groaned. 'Oh, no! What rotten luck—hey, Judith,

you wouldn't—you couldn't——'

'Yes, I could. Do you want me to?'

'Do I? Don't I just! That would be super. Hang on, I've got the number of a boatman at Lerwick. He'll bring you over.' She fumbled in her bag. 'Got a pen?'

She held another coin ready while her friend went for paper and pen, and gave her Dougall's number. 'How soon can you make it?'

'Well, I'll have to see my mother about minding the cats, and get my tickets fixed up. Can you phone me in the morning?'

'Of course. I'll be up at the crack of dawn—well, thereabouts. I don't think they have dawn up here. It never really goes dark——'

'Spare me the geographical details, dear. Think of your two bobs vanishing. Hey, can I call you back?'

'Yes. Good idea.' She peered at the number on the phone and read it out to her friend.

A few minutes later, walking away from the phone, Emma had a new spring to her step, a smile on her face. She knocked on the door at the Misses Murrays, loudly, and waited. It was late evening, but the rain had cleared and it was still light, and the world was a marvellous place to be in, and Skeila especially a lovely place to spend a peaceful holiday.

She went in to thank the two old women for their help and to tell them her news. She didn't stay long, as it was obvious that they were preparing to go to bed, but was made to promise that she would take Judith to see them the minute she arrived.

Then she set off to walk the two miles to Craig House. In the midst of her feeling of pleasure at Judith's imminent arrival was another, quite satisfying thought. She would like to see Greg Halcro's face when she told him her news.

30

Now he would have two women to contend with, not one. Everyone liked Judith. She was gentle, easygoing, a happy person who rarely argued or disagreed with anyone. It would be interesting to see how he acted towards her. That prickly aggression that so antagonized Emma would probably slide off Judith completely. Emma resisted the temptation to laugh out aloud. Oh yes, it would be interesting to see what Judith made of *him*, too. She was shrewd in her judgements, quick to size up someone's personality. How would she react? Emma found the question intriguing. One thing was sure—she would soon know.

She couldn't open the front door. She wore softly under her breath and tried again. Greg Halcro had done it, which should have eased the lock if only slightly. His Land-Rover was parked at the other side of the house, so he was at home. She did not want to ask him for help—unless there was no alternative—and she remembered something she had once read, and quickly opened her bag for her pencil. It was something to do with the lead, which was really graphite and would act as a lubricant on the lock. She had it now, and very carefully rubbed the pointed end of the key, praying that *he* would be engrossed in television—and then she looked around, because a dog's subdued woof sounded very near—and Greg Halcro was standing watching her.

'Having trouble?' he enquired, walking up. He had been out with the dogs. They collapsed in twin heaps, watchful eyes on their master as he strode over to Emma.

'Yes,' she answered shortly.

'Oh dear, oh dear,' he said. 'What are we going to do with you?'

Emma turned round slowly and looked up straight into that mocking face. 'Never mind,' she said. 'I have a friend coming in a day or two. She's very efficient. I'm sure that between us we'll manage very well.'

Just for a moment something flickered in his eyes, a certain darkness that crossed his features, then was gone. 'Really? May I have a key?' She handed it to him. 'Thanks. When is your friend arriving?'

'I don't know. I'm phoning in the morning.'

He opened the door and pushed it ajar, handing the key back to Emma. 'Couldn't she have come up with you?'

'No. She thought her husband was coming back from Canada and only just found out he's got to stay a while longer. So——' Emma shrugged. 'Now she's joining me. I've told her how wonderful it is up here,' she added, just to rub it in, 'and she can't *wait*.'

'Is she a model too?'

'No. She doesn't go out to work.' She pushed the door open wide. 'May I return your hospitality, Mr. Halcro? A cup of tea, or anything?' She knew he would refuse.

'No, thanks. I'll away and feed the dogs now. Goodnight, Miss Laing.'

'Goodnight.' She went in and closed the door. It was there, all the time, the latent hostility. There, but veiled. But Emma sensed it and wondered if it would be as obvious to Judith. She was more than ever pleased that her friend was able to come up to Skeila. In her calm way she would be able to assure Emma that the whole situation was partly due to her imagination. In a way, Emma hoped so. Her nerves were already raw from her encounter with Greg Halcro. Much more from him and she would lose her temper completely—and undoubtedly regret it afterwards.

She went into the kitchen and filled the kettle. A cup of coffee was what she needed. That, and a think. A think about a lot of things. The nice old ladies, her phone call to Judith, with its surprisingly pleasant result, Greg Halcro, her aggressive neighbour—and something else. Something that nagged at the back of her mind, but refused to become clear. A tiny incident, a casual word, but something not quite right. She didn't even know what it was.

Emma lay in bed much later. The window was wide open, it was still light and the air was cool and clean. She lay comfortably on her back, going over the events of the day in her mind. She was content, except for the one thing that still bothered her, that tiny inconsequential worry that refused to go away. With each minute that passed she became more sure that what was bothering her was something that had been said by Greg Halcro. But what? And then an image of his face, as it had been outside the house, came back to her. She had just told him that a friend was coming, noted his reaction, and a few seconds later he had asked: 'Is she a model too?'

Emma sat up in bed. That was it! 'Is she a model too?' The words seemed to echo around her. She had not told anyone of her job. Yet he knew. He *knew*. But he couldn't know. She put her hand to her forehead, trying to think clearly, going quickly over everything she had said to Dougall, to the two old ladies, in case it had been mentioned casually and then forgotten.

Slowly she lay back in bed and pulled the covers up. The sooner Judith came, the better. There was something wrong. She didn't know what it was, but she began to feel afraid of Greg Halcro.

Emma's travelling alarm clock shrilled at seven-thirty and woke her from a deep sleep. She groaned, reached out to switch off the bell and turned over again. She was comfortable and warm, and it was Saturday, so there was no need to get up...

And then she remembered. Judith! She had to phone her

and find out when she would be coming. Emma scrambled out of bed and went to the window. It was a glorious day outside. The sun shone, and gulls flew high over the cliffs, wheeling and gliding, their wings turning to silver in the light. She breathed deeply of the fresh salty air and went to have a wash. With any luck there would be sufficient hot water from the fire without having to heat any on the gas. Emma was determined not to waste that precious gas cylinder. Not until she knew if she could get more. That was something else to put on her list for the shop in the village.

She washed and dressed in comfortable jeans and sweater, and went downstairs. Her fears of the previous night seemed rather stupid in the clear light of day. But one thing she had decided—she would ask Greg Halcro how he knew she was a model. If she didn't, she knew the question would nag her in a way quite out of proportion to its importance.

She scribbled on the list in the kitchen—a steadily growing one with all the items that she needed—and hoped the store would be able to supply. After a quick breakfast of toast and tea, she went to find her flat shoes, put on her short furry jacket and set off walking. It was now nearly nine. Nothing stirred in Greg Halcro's house next door, and no smoke came from the chimney. Emma looked away and on towards the village. How nice it would be if she could ignore him completely. A wry smile curved her lips at that impossible thought.

Sheep scuttered away at her approach, and birds rose from their hiding places in the heather-covered ground and soared upwards. The road stretched ahead, narrow and winding, and soon the village would come into sight. There was something missing. Emma looked around her, taking in the green windswept grass, occasional boulders, the distant

34

glitter of a restless sea, and then realized what it was. There were no trees. An occasional stunted bush, but no tall elegant pines. The hills rose to her right, bleakly forbidding and windswept, but there was not a tree to be seen anywhere. There was undeniable beauty here, and she wondered what winter would be like.

It must be a lonely life for Greg Halcro. Perhaps he too left in the dark December months. Emma found her preoccupation with him annoying, yet he constantly returned to her thoughts. It would be, she reflected, as she walked briskly along, a relief when Judith arrived, in more ways than one.

The first houses came into sight, and the fishing boats. A couple of old women stood talking in a doorway and greeted her with a polite good day as she passed them on her way to the telephone. No doubt they already knew who she was, and where she was staying; a difference from London where everyone was too busy with their own affairs to concern themselves with strangers.

Judith was in. She was travelling up by plane on Monday morning to Aberdeen, and would be in Lerwick Tuesday.

'That's the earliest I can do it,' she assured Emma. 'My mother's going away for the weekend, so I'm taking the cats to her on Sunday night.'

'It'll give me a chance to get everything nice for you,' Emma answered, swallowing disappointment at the two-day delay. 'And don't forget your portable radio, will you?'

'I won't. How do you manage for lights?'

'I didn't need one last night, but there's an oil lamp in the kitchen. I'm going to the general store now. Keep your fingers crossed they sell paraffin.'

Judith laughed. 'I will. I'm looking forward to coming. Hey, how's Thing—you know, your neighbour?'

'Greg Halcro? He had to open the door for me last night

—the lock gets stuck. He gets me *mad*, just by his attitude, honestly.'

'Sounds fun—I can't wait to meet him. We should sort him out between us, don't worry.'

For a moment Emma was tempted to tell her of Greg's question, then decided not to. It was a waste of valuable phone time, and in any case seemed to be making a fuss about nothing. And by the time Judith arrived she would have solved the mystery anyway . . .

She went into the general store after her call was over, and ordered the things she needed. There was paraffin in stock, and Calor gas. Which prompted the awful suspicion —Greg Halcro must have known that fact, probably even bought his own gas cylinders there, so why had he not told Emma? It was another point to add to the growing list of her grievances against him. Mr. Grant assured her he would deliver the gas and paraffin later that day, and would he take her groceries too?

'I'll manage those, thanks,' Emma told him. She wanted to put everything away neatly, and make the house more home-like. It was odd how quickly she was beginning to like the place she had seen for the first time only the previous day. Difficult too for her to remember her acute feelings of dismay at her first sight of it.

The elderly helpful shopkeeper piled her groceries neatly in a cardboard box for her, and Emma left. She set off walking at a nice steady pace, but before she was away from the last houses, had to slow down. The box was quite heavy, and would have been easier if she had thought to get string tied round it, to enable her to carry it with her arm down. For a moment she considered returning to the shop and asking Mr. Grant to put everything with the gas to be delivered later. But the frozen fish for her lunch was at the bottom of the box, and he would think she was soft anyway . . .

She heard the engine's roar behind her and moved instinctively to the very edge of the road. It couldn't be—could it? But she realized now that the one thing missing from her neighbour's house when she set out had been the Land-Rover. She kept on walking, looking resolutely ahead, determined not to slow, or in any way to show that she hoped for a lift. For she didn't anyway—and he wouldn't stop for her, not if she was alone, only when she was with old ladies ...

'You'd better get in.' He was leaning out, and the engine rumbled, protesting at this unexpected halt, and Emma looked at him, then walked round the front to the passenger door, which he opened.

He took the box from her and put it in the back. 'Ready?'

'Yes, thank you.' The door slammed, they were off.

He drove along without speaking. Emma wondered where he had been. She hadn't heard or seen his Land-Rover go, and she had been up before eight. She would not ask, that was sure. There was one thing she had to find out though, and she waited until he was lifting out her box and said: 'Thank you for the lift. Please tell me something. How did you know I was a model?'

His back was towards her so that she couldn't see his face. He was carrying her box towards her front door, and he didn't stop or answer until he had put the groceries down on the step.

'You'd better give me your key,' he said, and held out his hand. 'How did I know you're a model?' He seemed amused. 'Aren't you?'

'Yes. But I never told you——'

'You didn't need to. It sticks out a mile. You walk differently, look different—it's an *air* about you—that's all.' And he shrugged, and held out his hand. 'Key?'

Emma had a helpless feeling. She didn't believe him—

37

she didn't know why—but her heart beat faster because there was no way she could challenge him without actually calling him a liar. And she was tempted to do that, but held her tongue. She looked into those cool dark grey eyes, and had the strangest feeling that he could read her thoughts. Quickly she bent her head and opened her bag. He took the key from her.

'You'll have to learn to open the door yourself,' he said. 'Or what will you do if I'm not here?'

'Then let me try now,' she retorted, 'or I'll never know, will I?' And she reached out her hand to take the key back from him. Something odd happened when their fingers inescapably touched at the hand-over, a sudden startling shock. Emma jerked her hand away and turned towards the door. And he began to laugh. She looked quickly round.

'Don't tell me I frighten you?' he said, and his mouth was smiling, but his eyes weren't. They were dark and watchful. And Emma shook her head.

'Don't be ridiculous,' she answered. 'Why should you think that?' But he was too close to the truth for her comfort.

# CHAPTER THREE

SATURDAY and Sunday passed quickly because Emma had plenty to do. Mr. Grant had come on the Saturday afternoon and showed her how to trim the wick and light the oil lamp. He stayed for a cup of tea and a talk, a kindly quietly spoken man who had lived on the island all his life and knew everyone and everything about it, including her next-door neighbour, about whom he seemed disposed to talk.

And Emma let him. Despite all her resolutions, she was deeply curious about the man next door.

'It is nice to have a neighbour for you, no doubt,' Mr. Grant said, fumbling in his pocket and digging out an ancient pipe. 'Eh, do you mind me smoking this?'

'Not at all,' Emma said. 'Another cup of tea, Mr. Grant?'

'If it's no trouble.' His voice followed her out to the kitchen. 'A strange man, your neighbour. He's not a native of these parts at all.'

'Really?' Emma handed him the steaming beaker. 'I imagined he was.'

'Ach no, it is only about the last six years he has been here. Mind, he may have come from one of the other islands, but he never speaks about himself, not at all,' and he shook his head, as if mildly surprised at that fact.

'He's writing a book about birds,' Emma told him, to see if that would trigger off anything.

'Oh yes, so I believe. Very interesting. There are many varieties of birds here, of course, a naturalist's paradise. Yes indeed, it would be interesting to see this book when it comes out,' and there was a certain expression on his face as

39

he said it that prompted Emma's question.

'What do you mean?'

'Aye well, he's been a very long time in the writing of it. Who knows when it will be finished?' And he nodded sagely and applied a match to his pipe and puffed vigorously.

'Perhaps books like that do take a long time,' Emma said.

'No doubt. No doubt. I wouldn't know myself. He has a beautiful camera. Ah!' and he sighed. 'Now if I had a camera like that I'd be taking photos all the time. It takes special film which I have to order for him. He must use a great deal of film for this book.'

He looked at his watch. 'Well, I'd best be away. My wife will be waiting with my meal. Don't forget now, Miss Laing, it's always a pleasure to see you in the shop when you come to the village, and perhaps you'll pop in for a cup of tea the next time?'

'I'd love to. Thank you.' Emma watched him go, driving away in a battered blue van of uncertain age and giving her a last wave before he was out of sight. She closed the door thoughtfully. It hadn't been his words so much as the way he had said them.

She wondered again what Judith would make of Greg Halcro.

On Monday Emma did a pile of washing in the sink. After she had hung the clothes out she looked ruefully at her hands. No doubt about it, some of the London gloss was wearing off since her arrival three days previously. There seemed no point in doing elaborate hairstyles on this windy isle. She had caught her shoulder-length blonde hair back in a blue silk headscarf, tied it in a bow, and looked about eighteen instead of twenty-three.

And make-up didn't seem so important here either. What had usually taken her anything up to half an hour—or even more, if she was going on a special modelling job—now took a few minutes; a swift smoothing on of lipstick, a touch of eye-pencil and shadow was all that she felt inclined to do.

She rubbed cream on her hands and went up to make her bed. A fire glowed brightly in the hearth and gleamed reflectively in the furniture. Everything was old, but good, and had been crying out for polish. Emma had bought a tin on the Saturday and used most of it on Sunday. She wondered if Judith would be surprised at this change in her. She was amazed at herself. Her flat in London was just a base, a place in which to sleep and store possessions, and a cleaner came twice a week so that Emma never had to do any housework. Yet here she felt a certain pride in her surroundings. She was not sure how much of it was the desire to let Greg Halcro see that she wasn't so easily deferred—in fact she had the sudden desire to invite him in, and let him see the difference for himself. For difference there was—subtle and not easily defined. The house was no longer an empty cold shell, it had become a home. Emma ran her hand over the smooth surface of the sideboard. She regretted never having come up here before. Her life had been too full to even think of it. And what would Robert have made of it? She didn't know. He was very much a city man—the country bored him. With a sudden shock of realization, Emma realized that she hadn't really known him at all. And then she sensed that perhaps it was because, after all, there had been no great depth to him. Maybe Judith, in her quiet way, was right. She had never liked him—yet had hidden it well because Emma was her friend. They would, she decided, have to have a talk about him.

Emma looked at the curtains. A drab brown, they would

be better for a wash too. She looked at her hands, sighed and went to get a chair to stand on.

Late evening. The lamp was lit, the fire dying down, and Emma yawned and put her book down. Tomorrow Judith would arrive, and then there would be long walks. In a way, it would be the true beginning of the holiday. She had been down to the beach that afternoon, seen the huge jagged rocks thrusting up cruelly from the sea, and the boat moored in a quiet inlet, a superb boat with the name 'Maria' painted on it. She wondered if it was Greg's and had stood quietly looking at it for several minutes. She knew little about boats, but this looked good, a sleek expensive craft that bobbed gently at its mooring, and looked powerful enough to go anywhere.

She thought of the boat as she went to draw the curtains. She had seen nothing of her neighbour that day, but his dogs had been out running across the dark heather, and she had heard him whistle them back. She pulled the clean dry curtains together, pleased that she had washed them: the drab brown had gone away to reveal soft dark gold, a warm glowing colour that suited the room. She was looking forward to seeing Judith's reaction when she first stepped into the house.

Perhaps it was excitement at seeing a friend that kept Emma from sleep. Whatever it was, she was still fully awake at one a.m. and went down to make herself a cup of tea. The kitchen curtains were not drawn together, and it was light enough for her not to bother with the lamp. She lit the gas and waited for the kettle to boil, and glanced towards the window because there had come a faint sound.

A dark figure passed, and she froze momentarily. Had she bolted the door? He hadn't stopped, there was no hesitation. Emma went over to the window and looked out, her teeth biting into her lower lip. Greg Halcro strode towards the cliff, and carried what looked like a camera slung over his shoulder. Even as Emma watched, he began to scramble down and vanished. Without waiting to think why she was doing it, Emma ran upstairs to the back bedroom, there to see better. Had he gone to his boat?

The moon shone on the water and turned it to molten silver, and there was utter silence everywhere. And then she saw it, an ebony sleek shape sliding from the shadows of the cliff and thrusting through that silver and black water. The motor was almost silent, there were no lights, and it was like watching a film. She looked until the boat vanished and went downstairs. So Greg Halcro was out on a moonlight ride—and why not? Perhaps he was going fishing. But it was the secrecy of it all that bothered Emma. It had been almost—sinister, to see the boat with not one single light on. What reason could he have?

She woke on Tuesday morning with that faint sense of unease remaining, not remembering why until she went down to the kitchen and looked out of the window. And then it all came back. Emma unbolted the back door and went out. The wind nearly swept her off her feet and she gasped at its force as she ran across dry springy turf to the cliff. The boat was gone still. She looked back at his silent sleeping house. His Land-Rover was parked outside, and if she hadn't seen him go she would have assumed that he was still abed. Hugging her arms to her, she ran quickly back to the house and shut the back door. It was nearly eight. Judith would be at Lerwick. Perhaps she was even now phoning Dougall. Soon she would be here. And then nothing would seem so mysterious at all, for Judith had a refreshing sense of humour, and together they would be able to laugh at Emma's stupid imaginings.

She prepared her breakfast. Toast was no longer enough, for Emma's appetite seemed to be increasing daily, and it should have worried her, for her figure was an essential part of her assets; but it didn't. London seemed so very far away. There would be time to diet when she returned. A few days on yoghurt and salad would do the trick. She carried the plate of bacon and egg to the table and sat down.

She had finished it and was drinking her coffee when the knock came at the front door. For a moment, a vision of Judith standing on the doorstep with her suitcases came to mind. But that was utterly impossible!

It was Greg Halcro. Holding an enormous fish. 'Hello,' he said. 'I thought you might like this for your lunch. I've just been out on a fishing trip.'

'Come in.' Emma stood back. She had dressed in slim-fitting grey trousers and red sweater, and her hair was loose. His eyes travelled swiftly down her, and he smiled. 'Your friend arrives today, doesn't she?'

'Yes. Thanks for the fish. Er—what is it?'

He was so tall, he seemed to fill that small living room. Emma was relieved that she had tidied up before going to bed, for he was looking round, taking it all in, she knew that. 'Mackerel—very tasty fried. You know how to fillet it, of course?'

'Actually no,' she admitted. 'I've never tried. But I'm sure I'll manage.' It was different in daylight. *He* was different too. Almost as if he were trying to be civil.

And Emma responded. She had known fear of him, but she would try never to let it show. Not ever. It was fatal to let anyone know you were afraid of them, a dog, a burglar —or this big dark disturbing man who went out at night in a silent boat and then brought her a fish—as if nothing at all was amiss. Perhaps it wasn't.

44

'I'd better do it for you, then, hadn't I?' He was striding through to the kitchen, and she followed. He would notice the difference there too, if he was half as observant as she suspected. For she had spent several hours the previous day washing down paintwork and floor until everything shone. But if he did, he said nothing about it, merely dumped the fish in her sink. 'Got a sharp knife?' he asked.

'Yes. Here.' She passed him one and he looked at it.

'That's no good. I'll use mine.' He bent, reached in the thick wellingtons he wore and produced a knife. Razor sharp, it glinted wickedly in the light and she swallowed a gasp of dismay.

He held it up. 'My *skean dhu*,' he said, 'sharp enough to slice a hair in half.'

'I believe you. Isn't it dangerous—there?' she nodded towards his feet.

He laughed. His teeth were white and strong. 'It's in a sheath,' he told her. 'I won it off a Highlander.' He grinned again. 'It's very handy.'

She didn't want to know what for. 'I'll get a plate,' she said. 'There's coffee in the pot. Will you have a cup?'

'Please. No sugar.' She poured it out and watched him work, admiring the efficiency, the swift glint of the blade as it sliced into the fish, his complete absorption in his task. He had just returned from the sea, and it must have been cold, for he wore a thick dark jacket over his sweater, black trousers and sea-boots. His hair needed a comb, and he needed a shave and Emma suddenly wondered, quite absurdly, what it would feel like to be kissed by him now. She turned quickly away lest it show on her face.

What a *stupid* thought to have! How utterly ridiculous! She poured herself out another cup of coffee, more for something to do than because she wanted one.

'That's it. Got an old newspaper?'

45

'Wait. I bought one on Saturday.' He wrapped the bones and skin up and put them in the waste bin.

'Thank you. It looks delicious.' She put the white pieces of fish on to a plate and into the food cupboard.

'Coat it with flour and fry quickly.'

'Yes. I'll buy some more this morning when I go to meet Judith.'

He turned round, leaning negligently against the sink as he drank his beaker of coffee. 'And what are you going to do with yourselves for the next—how long are you here for, by the way?'

She was about to reply: 'Two weeks' which would have been the truth, but something made her say instead: 'As long as I want. Why?' Because he had been so obviously trying to get rid of her before, maybe still was, and she wanted to see his reaction.

'You'll soon get bored here. There's very little to do for a city girl like yourself.' And then he added: 'Besides, won't they want you back?'

She didn't like his tone. She didn't like the way he said 'city girl' as if it were faintly insulting. She didn't like *him*, come to that.

'I'm freelance. I don't easily get bored, and I'm not sure what you mean by city girl, Mr. Halcro.' Emma stood there, tall and graceful, and he wasn't going to get away with anything if she could help it.

He winced. 'Ouch! They spark fire when you're angry. Did you know?'

'What do?'

'Those eyes of yours. Boy, I wouldn't like to be in the way when you're really mad!'

Emma took a deep breath. This was ridiculous. He'd only been in the house five minutes, they'd started off in a perfectly civilized manner, and now things were degenerating into a fight. 'You're very insulting!' she breathed. 'Has no one ever told you that?'

He seemed to be considering it. 'I don't think so,' he answered, after a few moments. 'What did I say to insult you?'

'You must be *joking*! It's been one long insult ever since I arrived. Even before I met you, it was "young Greg won't like this", and I thought, who the hell is young Greg—and then I met you, and they were quite right—you didn't like it, and you made it perfectly obvious—and let me tell you *this*, young Greg Halcro, this is *my* house, and I'll stay here as long as I like, whether it suits you or not!' And she nodded, just to emphasise the last word, and took a deep breath, then let it out.

Greg Halcro gave a long low whistle. His broad mouth widened into a smile.

'God! What a temper! Have you finished? Can I speak now?'

'I shouldn't imagine you letting anything stop you talking, if you wanted.'

'Then I'll tell you something. When your great-uncle died, I wrote to the solicitors trying to buy the house. They replied that the new owner intended coming up very soon and no doubt I could talk it over with her. That was two years ago.' He paused. 'It's a shame to leave a nice house like this to rot—but that's what you've done, isn't it? And I dare say you'll go away again when your holiday is over, and that will be that for how long?—another three years?'

Emma was silent. The solicitors had told her of an offer, and she had refused it, intending as she did to come soon. And Greg Halcro added softly. 'Lost your tongue now?'

'I don't have to explain my actions to you.'

'No, quite true. You don't. Did I say you did?'

She ignored that. 'Anyway, what could you want two

47

houses for? You can only live in one.' And she smiled. She had him *there*.

'I know that. But I often have friends visiting. These houses are quite small. I need more room, that's all. And it would have been used.' His dark eyes gleamed, as if daring her to go further.

Emma had a strangely helpless feeling. Men didn't treat her in the way this one was doing. She was accustomed to admiring attention, not this hard aggression, this utter resistance. She took a deep breath. 'I'm sure you have plenty to do,' this glancing pointedly at his empty beaker. 'I know I have, before *my* friend arrives.'

'And I'd better leave? Good point.' He emptied and rinsed his beaker under the tap, then washed the knife blade before sliding it back into its place of concealment. 'After all, we wouldn't want a fight, would we?' Hard eyes held hers in a glance of dark mystery. 'Not as we're neighbours.'

'You don't seem to be doing too badly so far,' she retorted, knowing she should just keep quiet, let him go, but quite unable to do so. He had a certain effect on her ...

He did a startling thing, reached out his hand and ran it down her cheek, and laughed softly. 'You're a worthy opponent, anyway,' he said. Emma knocked his hand away. She was breathing hard.

'Don't touch me!'

'Mmm, nice soft skin. Look after it. The wind plays havoc with it hereabouts. You don't want to go back all weatherbeaten, do you?' He was laughing at her. 'That would never do—not in your job——'

'Get out!' She clenched her fists in helpless anger. Oh, for the strength to hit him——!

'I'm going, little hellcat. Hey, is this friend of yours like you?'

'Get——'

'I heard you the first time. Get out. Yes, I'm going. But first——' he stopped. She didn't know what was in his mind. She couldn't have imagined what would happen, not in a thousand years. He bent his head, put his hands on her upper arms, and kissed her.

She was too startled to move, to struggle, to do anything. She just stood there and let him do it. And then he was gone, moving through the living room, opening the front door. 'That's for the fish,' he said, and the door closed after him. Laughter echoed after him.

Emma put her hand to her lips. They still tingled. She had wondered briefly what it would be like to be kissed by Greg Halcro. Now she knew—rough, disturbing, not gentle. But like nothing that had ever happened before. And how quickly he moved when he chose to! The imprint of his mouth still lingered as he was away, and out. Then Emma began to laugh. How utterly outrageous he was! And what a thing to tell Judith. One thing was certain—he wouldn't take her by surprise again. Or so she thought.

It was like waiting for someone to arrive on a train—only the setting was beautifully different and exciting. Emma had visited the two old ladies, and been to the shop, leaving her box of groceries to be collected on her way back. And now she sat on a flat rock on the shore and waited. It was a good day for just sitting there. The wind had died down to a gentle breeze that teased her hair, and with the shelter of the rocks behind her, the sun's rays warmed her skin, turning it softly to gold.

The sea stretched endlessly away, and the horizon was a sharp flat line, completely empty of anything at all. Emma had patience. There was a sense of timelessness about everything. There was no hurry, no urgent rush to be anywhere, no appointments to keep. Nothing.

And then a speck appeared, and she knew who it was. It grew larger; a boat speeding across from Lerwick, coming straight here. She had to blink and shade her eyes, for the sun dazzled on the deceptively calm-looking sea. It would not be calm out there. She hoped that Judith wasn't feeling seasick.

The boat became recognizable, and the tiny dot at the helm, and she stood up and walked along the beach, kicking at the tiny pebbles, looking up again to wave as a second figure became visible, then recognizable. Judith waved back. Perhaps she wasn't feeling bad at all. Emma smiled at the thought. She hoped not. Lunch was planned, and if Judith was as starving as she herself had been shortly after her arrival, it would not be wasted.

The boat made a graceful curving turn and came gently to rest, and Dougall boomed: 'Good day to you, Miss Laing. We are safely here.'

'Good day, Dougall.' Then she was hugging Judith, tall curly-haired Judith, with the hidden laughter in her eyes, and Judith was exclaiming:

'Thank God! Dry land at last. You look very well Emma. This place must suit you.'

'Wait till you've been here a while. I'm eating like a horse—honestly, I'm getting worried.'

'Hmm.' Judith surveyed her critically. 'You never ate enough before, in my opinion. So hurray for Skeila. Gosh, talking about food, I'm starving!'

Dougall lifted out the two cases and a small sack. 'I'm away to the store,' he told them. 'Will I take these cases?'

'Please, Dougall. I've got some things to collect.' They walked along the stony road and Dougall told them about his adventures on a fishing trip recently, but Emma only half listened, for she was already planning the things she had to tell her friend.

50

Mr. Grant offered them a lift, if they were prepared to wait until he had sorted the mail, so they went back to visit the Misses Murray as Emma had promised, days ago, and again that morning. Judith looked round as they walked the short distance from the store. 'I like it here,' she said. 'It's just as I pictured it, somehow. What's the house like?'

Emma gave a little secret smile. 'Wait and see,' she said. 'I got a shock when I first saw it—but I think it's improved.'

Judith gave her a long shrewd look. 'You're *different*—I don't know why, or in what way, but you are.'

Emma laughed. 'In four days? Impossible!'

'No, I mean it.' Judith joined in the laughter, and then they were at the red door, with the geranium on the window-ledge beside it, and the subject was left.

There were three letters for Emma, forwarded from her flat by her cleaner. She looked briefly at them and put them in her bag. She recognized the writing on one. Robert's. There would be time to read it later. Mr. Grant dropped them near the house. He was going on to deliver mail and groceries to an outlying cottage a few miles on. They thanked him and watched him drive away, then set off up the short rough track to Craig House.

'Is that the dreaded Greg's house at the end?' Judith asked, as they neared the three cottages.

'Yes. That's his Land-Rover. He must be in. I bet he's watching us,' Emma answered. Yet there was no sign of movement at any window. It was just a feeling she had, a prickly sensation at the back of her neck.

'Hmm. I'm looking forward to meeting him,' said Judith.

'And I've got a lot to tell you, believe me.' Emma hoped he couldn't lip-read. Not that she cared really . . .

'As long as we can eat while you're telling me. Honestly, Emma, it must be this air or something. I'm *starving*!'

51

'Here we are.' Emma opened the door and they went in. Emma watched Judith's face, and was not disappointed at her friend's reaction.

'Oh, *Emma*! What a lovely little place!' The fire threw yellow darts of flame up the chimney, the furniture gleamed softly, and sun slanted across the carpet, and the room welcomed them like an old friend.

'You should have seen it when I arrived. My heart sank the first time I came in. All dark and dank. I felt like turning tail!'

Judith laughed. 'I believe you. You must have worked hard—and *that* I would have liked to have seen!'

'Don't be so cheeky! Hey, do you know something? I enjoyed it. I never thought the day would dawn when I'd enjoy housework, but it gives you a nice satisfying glow to see the colours emerge from the dullness—and something else,' and Emma frowned thoughtfully, 'I've just realized I wanted to show Greg Halcro——' and she smiled.

'He had such a superior look about him when he saw my face, a sort of "I'll bet she's a useless female" look—and more—that it was like a challenge to me.' She was moving towards the kitchen as she spoke. 'Come on, we'll eat, and I'll tell you all about him—and is there a lot to tell.'

Because she had already planned lunch before he brought the fish, she had decided to save that for their tea. Remembering her own feelings when she had smelt the steak and kidney pie at the old ladies' house, Emma had done the same for them both, surprising herself as she opened the oven to see the rich golden crust, steam gently rising, the aroma.

'I don't believe it! I never knew you could cook!'

Emma gave her friend a severe look. 'Any more and you'll be getting the next boat back to the mainland!'

She had prepared carrots and potatoes, left them gently

52

simmering, and they too were ready. She felt quite pleased with herself.

'Right.' Judith picked up knife and fork with a satisfied sigh. 'I'll eat. You talk.'

So Emma began the story with her arrival, those first warning mentions of 'young Greg', her reactions at their first meeting, and afterwards, finishing with his visit just a couple of hours previously that had started off so well and ended so startlingly.

'... And then...' she paused dramatically, an impish sense of humour sparking at the sight of Judith's rapt face.

'Yes, yes. *What?* Go on, do.' She had even stopped eating.

'And then he took hold of me, and kissed me.' And Emma looked demurely down at her lunch, and sliced a piece of potato in two.

There was complete silence. Emma looked up, and Judith smiled slowly.

'Beautiful,' she murmured. 'Just beautiful! I can't wait to meet him.'

Emma burst out laughing. 'You should see your face! I've told you—he's *awful*. The cheek of the man—and then to cap it all, as he went out, he said: "That's for the fish." I could have thrown something—but he'd gone.'

'Hmm, knows how to make an exit too. Are you sure he wants to get rid of you? He sounds as if he fancies you——'

'Never! After all I've told you? You're joking. I've got a feeling he's up to no good—but I don't know what. He couldn't be a smuggler, could he?'

'Oh, Emma! You've been reading too many thrillers.'

'Well, there was something in the way Mr. Grant spoke about his writing—as if he didn't believe it either. And I've been in his house. Surely there'd have been something there

53

—papers, photos, a typewriter?'

'He's got two bedrooms, hasn't he? I dare say he uses one of those as a study.'

'You're so practical,' Emma grumbled. 'No imagination at all.'

'Just realistic, love. People just don't live next door to smugglers or secret agents or whatever. Let me see him, then I'll let you know what I think.'

Emma stood up to take their empty plates away. 'Anyway, never mind Greg Halcro. I'm glad you're here. We're going to have a super time, I can feel it in my bones. And you must tell me all about John and why he had to stay in Canada.'

She poured boiling water into the pot to make coffee, and the two girls went into the front room to drink it, and to talk.


They set out for a long walk, to explore the island later on. Judith saw Emma lift the walking stick from its place by the back door and raised her eyebrows.

'Getting old, dear?' she enquired.

'It's for the birds,' Emma answered. 'The ones hereabouts have nasty habits, like swooping down on people occasionally.'

'I don't believe it!' and Judith laughed.

'I'm not sure if I do either, but I'd hate to find out the hard way. We'll see.'

They struck out away from the sea towards higher ground. The sky was a clear pale blue with few clouds, and the sun's heat was tempered by a cool breeze which pulled at their hair. For a while they walked in companionable silence, with only the roar of the sea to keep them company. Sheep grazed, ignoring them completely, and when they had reached a high point, Judith stopped and put her hand on Emma's arm.

'Look down there,' she said. 'I wish I'd brought my camera. Why didn't you tell me?'

Emma looked. They both stood quite still at the sight which lay below them in a hollow, fearful to break the spell. Several ponies were grazing, miniatures, long-maned and tailed, and as small as young foals, but plump and perfectly formed.

'Oh, aren't they gorgeous!'

'They'll run if we go any nearer—you can tell now, one is watching us, ready to move away.' Further on was a whitewashed cottage with grey tiled roof and several out-buildings. And further still, the sea, mistily distant with other islands seen as faint grey smudges in the water.

'Oh, Emma,' Judith whispered. 'I didn't realize just how beautiful it was here.'

'Nor did I,' Emma admitted. She had to add: 'I'd have been up before if I'd known. You can unwind here—you can't do that in London.'

Judith gave her a long shrewd glance. 'And Robert? Have you got over him yet?'

Emma looked blankly at her. 'Robert! I had a letter from him. I forgot!'

'You've just answered my question, love.' She shook her head. 'No, sorry, I shouldn't have asked. You don't just get over a broken engagement in five minutes——'

'But I'd *forgotten*, don't you see?' Emma had the oddest sensation. 'I wouldn't have thought it possible. All the hurt of the past few weeks—I'd have ripped it open straight-away in London, but I just stuffed it in my bag, because it didn't seem quite so important——' she put her hand to her cheek.

'Never mind. You'll read it when you get back, and I'll get on with my unpacking.' Judith was skilfully changing the subject. Emma sensed this, and let her. 'Where will I sleep?'

'There's a bed in the back bedroom. I've aired all the bedding, and it feels quite comfortable.'

'Good. What's the hot water situation?'

'Oh, it's heated by the fire. There's usually plenty for a bath.'

'Lovely. Just like home.' They started to walk down the steep slope, moving slowly to avoid startling the ponies. In vain, for they skittered away at the girls' approach and stopped a few hundred yards further away, looking at them with wary eyes and tossing heads.

As they approached the farm, the door was opened and they saw an elderly woman waving. For a moment Emma was tempted to look over her shoulder, in case there was someone behind them ...

'She's waving to us,' whispered Judith, returning the wave.

'Good day. A nice afternoon,' the woman called, and the girls scrambled down the last few yards of rocky slope, and Emma answered.

'Yes, lovely.'

'Would you like a cup of tea?'

They looked quickly at one another. 'Yes, please.' The yard was swept clean, and looked unused. The doorway was low, making them instinctively duck their heads as they went in to a warm living room where a fire burned brightly with a kettle steaming merrily away on a hob.

'I saw you coming through the glasses,' the old woman explained. 'I thought you might like a drink after your walk. Sit down, it won't be a moment.'

There were binoculars on the low wide window-ledge, and it reminded Emma of the ones she had seen in Greg Halcro's house, in a similar place. The sea was behind the

56

farmhouse, at the other side. You could hear it all the time, an ever-constant presence. There would be plenty to look at from that other side, the ever changing moods of the wild water, the birds, boats.

And distantly came another sound, quietly intrusive, growing nearer; an engine. The old woman reappeared, her face lit up with surprise. 'My, this is my day for visitors,' she said. 'Young Greg is just arriving.'

# CHAPTER FOUR

'I DON'T believe it!' Emma muttered as the old lady bustled out.

'It appears to be true,' Judith calmly murmured in reply. 'So you'd better wipe that light of battle from your eyes.'

They heard the other, front door opening, Greg's deep voice, the old woman's in reply. Then he walked in. And Emma quelled a ridiculous flutter in the region of her heart at the sight of him. He was carrying a fish, was clearly expecting to see someone—but perhaps not them, for his face had, for a moment, a look of dark surprise—which was instantly banished as though it had never been.

'Hello,' he said, and looked at them both. Emma turned to Judith, coolness returning. 'Judith, this is Mr. Halcro, my next door neighbour—Mrs. Roberts.' She watched them shaking hands, exchange the conventional meaningless greetings, and inside her was the unspoken question: 'I wonder what she makes of him?'

'Oh, you know each other. How nice.' The old lady was nodding happily, wiping her hands on her brightly patterned pinafore.

'Yes, Mrs. Stevenson, we're neighbours, at least Miss Laing and I are,' and Greg turned from the old woman to give Emma a smile. 'I've brought you this fish—shall I take it out to the kitchen for you?'

'How nice. I hoped you **would. Yes,** please do. And I'll make more tea for you. You **just arrived** in time...' Their voices faded as they went **out of the** room, and Judith turned to Emma and pursed her lips in a silent whistle.

58

'What?' Emma whispered.

'He's big, isn't he?' Her mouth trembled with the effort not to smile. 'Fancy being kissed——'

'Ssh!' Emma was frightened he might return suddenly. She had ceased to be surprised at anything he did any more. And in any case he probably had radar-sharp ears, and could hear through three-foot-thick walls ...

'Aye, he's just cleaning it for me,' Mrs. Stevenson handed them each a fragile china cup and saucer. 'He'll not be a moment.'

Judith, as if sensing Emma's consternation, took over the conversational reins.

'Do you live alone here, Mrs. Stevenson?' she asked.

The old woman was lifting a tin of biscuits down from a shelf and didn't reply for a moment. She opened the tin and held it out.

'I have my son Ian comes home when he can from the——'

'That's done. I've put the fish away in your fridge.' Greg had come in suddenly and Emma wondered if he had been listening. It was as if he had interrupted the old woman deliberately. But for what reason? Perhaps it was her imagination, working overtime again whenever he was concerned. 'Shall I pour my tea out now?'

'Indeed and you will not! After fetching me that lovely fish for my supper? Sit you down, and talk to these young ladies,' and she went out.

'Mrs. Stevenson's son works on another island and comes home most weekends—when he can,' he said, quite pleasantly.

'Oh, what does he do?' Emma hadn't been interested before. Now she was.

He shrugged. 'Some sort of office job for one of these American firms—connected with the oil rigs, I think. And what do you think of Skeila, Mrs. Roberts?'

Judith smiled at him. 'I like it very much. There's a very peaceful atmosphere that makes a terrific contrast from London's bustle. Have you lived here long?'

'A few years. I'm writing a book about the birds hereabouts.'

'Really? How fascinating!' Judith appeared to be terribly interested, which Emma thought was rather odd, for she had never heard her friend express the slightest knowledge of feathered creatures before. 'I suppose there are plenty of varieties to study here?'

'Oh yes. Dozens.' His face gave nothing away.

'How far are you on with your book?' Then Emma knew, and a tingle of anticipation ran up her spine.

'I'm not doing so badly. Of course, there's a lot of research involved, and a bird sanctuary on another island a few miles away. But you need patience to photograph some kinds in their natural habitat. They resent strangers—and I can't say I blame them.' And he glanced fleetingly at Emma, and smiled.

'Have you got a publisher interested yet?' Judith's expression was so innocent that it would have fooled Emma, if she hadn't *known*.

'I've had talks with a friend in the game in London, but you know publishers—they're cagey people most of the time. Don't like to commit themselves.'

'Oh, I know.' Judith gave a sympathetic grimace. 'I used to work for one, ages ago, before I married. Would I know your friend?'

'I doubt it—he's not been there long—ah! thank you.' This as Mrs. Stevenson came in with his tea. He stood up to take the cup from her. 'I think I'm in your chair. I'll move over here,' and he went to sit by the window. The light was behind him, and his face was in shadow, but he

60

could see them clearly. And now he was doing the talking, leading the conversation, steering it cleverly but subtly away from any questions that concerned him as he said to the old woman:

'Is the television working still?'

'Oh yes! It's been fine since you mended it properly. Just fine,' and she nodded.

'I'm glad to hear it. You must let me know if you have any more trouble, and I'll try and fix it. But it's rather old, I'm afraid, and sometimes ...'

They listened, and joined in, and it was all very pleasant and casual, having tea and shortcakes in this old house, all part of their holiday, and something to remember when they were away back home in England. On the surface, that was. Yet Emma knew there were undercurrents, and was sure that Judith, with her sensitivity, was equally aware of them. There would be a lot to talk about, she thought, as she refused a third biscuit, when they were at Craig House again. There was time, plenty of time.

They went back along the shore in front of Mrs. Stevenson's house because she had told them it was a good safe walk, and they would enjoy it. Greg had not left with them, but he said goodbye pleasantly enough after they had thanked the old woman for her hospitality and been invited to return any time they wished.

For a few minutes they walked along the gritty shingle in silence. There was too much to be said, but it was as if they both instinctively wanted to get a safe distance from the house before they began.

Judith spoke first. She had looked back briefly, but both house and Land-Rover were hidden by rugged cliffs. She stopped and turned to Emma.

'Well!' she said.

61

'Is that all you can say?'

Judith shook her head. 'I don't know where to start—but I'll tell you one thing. There *is* something mysterious about that man. It's definitely not your imagination.'

Emma pulled a face in mock relief. 'So I'm not dotty after all, you mean?'

Judith laughed. 'I never thought you were. I just thought you were taking him too seriously—now I'm not so sure.' She picked up a pebble and flung it into the sea. 'He's a fascinating man, though.'

'Huh!'

Her friend gave Emma a knowing, shrewd look. 'Come off it! You don't fool me—you know damn well he is. Oh, you may not like him—I can even understand that—but you can't ignore him.'

'Hardly,' agreed Emma, 'the size of him.'

'Not just that either. There's—I don't know—something about him. I've not sorted it out yet, but I will.'

'And do you get the feeling he not only doesn't want us, but is hiding something?'

'Well——' Judith looked worried. 'I was looking for it, if you know what I mean—I suppose that's why I started asking him about his book—I wasn't too obvious, was I?' she finished anxiously.

Emma laughed. 'No! You really did sound fascinated in a genuine way.'

'That's a relief. I'd hate it if he'd thought anything was wrong. But he didn't tell us much, did he?'

'Precisely,' said Emma drily. 'Next to nothing, when you think it over. And he changes subjects very nicely when he wants to.'

'Mmm, yes. Especially when Mrs. Stevenson was beginning to tell us about her son.'

'So you noticed that too?' Emma asked. 'I thought there

was something funny about that, but I couldn't see why.'

'Nor could I. Unless they're both in the smuggling business together!'

'Oh, Judith, thank goodness you're here. Think of me—alone—with him driving me mad! At least we'll keep each other sane. And I won't be frightened of him——'

'Frightened? You weren't really, were you?'

'I don't know,' Emma said slowly. She hadn't intended that to come out. 'There have been one or two times when I felt——' she hesitated, then shook her head. 'Yes, I suppose I have. He has such a hard look about him at times—just a glimpse, but it's there—he's ruthless, for all that deceptively quiet air when he's talking to people like Mrs. Stevenson or the Misses Murray.'

'Yes, I think you're right. And his eyes seem to go right through you, as if he can read your thoughts——'

'He probably can. Funny how he should land up there so soon after us. Perhaps he was watching us through binoculars, and knew where we were heading.'

'A Peeping Tom? Ugh!' Judith pulled a face, then laughed. 'No, I'm sure he wouldn't do that. It's just coincidence. We're both getting carried away with this new neighbour of yours. I vote we *forget* him.'

'Agreed.' And Emma nodded. Ahead of them were two grey stone buildings standing quite alone and forlorn, facing the sea. They knew they were empty even before they neared them. The first was a house, its windows gaping bleakly out to the water, the second with larger arched windows could have been a school. They walked up to the schoolhouse, and Emma touched the door handle—and the door swung slowly open.

Desks were there, and pictures hung on the walls, childish paintings covered in dust, tattered. Judith whispered: 'I bet no one's been in here for years.'

And then Emma knew something that she should have realized ages before. She turned to Judith. 'That's it!' she exclaimed. 'I knew there was something missing. Since I've been here I've not seen one child. Not one. Or even,' she added, 'any young adults. They're all old people on this island.'

'Except for one,' Judith said drily. 'Or have you forgotten him already?'

'Yes, but he's not an islander—he's only been here a few years. All the natives are over fifty—at least.'

Judith nodded. 'I've not met them all, but I'm willing to bet you're right. How odd!'

They walked round the dusty classroom, lifting a desk lid occasionally to see if anything remained, but all traces of children's occupation had disappeared—save for those forlorn pictures still adorning the walls, and in a corner a child's glove. Judith picked it up and put it on a desk. 'How sad,' she said. Emma knew what she meant. She was standing by the teacher's desk and she lifted up the lid of that—and there was a dog-eared book inside. She lifted it out. '*The Vikings*,' it said.

She smiled and held it up for Judith to see. 'How appropriate,' she murmured. Judith came over to take the book from her and leaf through its tattered pages.

'I don't follow you,' she said, smiling.

'Him—Greg—he's like a Viking. A dark Viking.'

'Your dark Viking,' Judith said very softly.

'What?'

'Oh—nothing,' but she grinned as she turned away.

Emma put the book back and closed the desk lid. That was that. 'This place depresses me,' she said.

Judith seemed as if about to say something. She spun round on her heel. There was a light in her eyes, and Emma looked at her, puzzled.

64

'It's no good. I've been dying to tell you,' she said.

Emma's eyes widened. 'Judith, what is it?'

'I think I'm expecting!'

'A *baby*?'

Judith laughed. 'What else?'

'Oh, Judith, I'm so pleased!' Emma went over and impulsively hugged her friend. 'And you've been keeping it secret! You dark horse!'

Judith shook her head, laughing now. 'It's not *certain*—but yes, I'm pretty sure. It was just—coming here, somehow, seeing this empty classroom, so forlorn-looking, I just wanted to tell you, all of a sudden. I would have done anyway, before the holiday was over, but now seemed the right moment somehow. I don't know why.'

'How marvellous. And I dragged you all the way up here —oh dear! That rough boat! Are you sure you're all right?'

'I'm fine, honestly. If there'd been any doubt I'd have told you, never fear. And don't start to fuss me. I'm as strong as a horse, really.'

'Mmm,' Emma looked doubtful. 'I don't know. I have a certain responsibility now. Bags of eggs and milk and cheese for you now—and early nights——'

'Stop! Please.' Judith shook her head, the laughter spilling out. 'I'll be sorry I told you in a minute.' They were going towards the door, leaving the dusty deserted place behind, shutting the door after them, walking away along the beach. And now there was a new, far more interesting topic to talk over. Greg Halcro receded to the back of Emma's mind. Receded, but not disappeared, for somehow that became increasingly difficult with each hour that passed. She couldn't imagine why.

They ate the fish for tea, and it was delicious, and afterwards, with the radio switched on, Judith wrote to her husband to tell him about her journey and arrival on Skeila, and Emma at last, and with a strange reluctance, opened Robert's letter.

She stood by the window to read it, her back to Judith, who appeared too engrossed in what she was writing to bother anyway.

The bold black writing on stark white paper was so typically Robert. She looked at the address on the envelope for a few moments before taking out the sheet, and just for an instant saw his face as it had been in the last few bitter seconds of their final quarrel. Tall, fair and handsome, his mouth had been twisted with unhappiness as he had flung that hurtful accusation at her: 'You're not a woman—you're a machine. All you can think about is your modelling.'

'And what about you?' she'd flung back. 'Isn't your job important? You talk about it enough.'

'It's different for a man. This is my life, my career. I'll be a partner in the advertising agency in less than two years, the way I'm going now——'

'For heaven's sake—we're not still living in the Victorian age, you know! My job's important too. I don't just intend to give it up like that when we get married. I like my independence——'

'Then you don't love me enough?'

'I didn't say that!' But even as she said the words, she had looked at him, and wondered. Did she love him? She was no longer sure. She didn't even know if she knew what love was—and at the memory, in sudden anguish, she turned now to Judith and asked:

'What's it like to love someone?'

Judith looked up, startled, from her letter. 'Heavens, Emma, what is it, love? Why do you ask that? What has

Robert said?'

Emma shook her head. The letter was still tightly folded in her hand. 'I haven't read it yet. I don't know. I just had a memory of our last awful row, where Robert accused me of not loving him—and I suddenly realized that he might have been right. Perhaps I didn't. Oh, I was attracted to him, and we had fun, but I never really got to know him, it was all on the surface, all bright and brittle—no depth. You love John, I know that. Tell me.'

Judith closed the notepad and gave a slow, soft smile. 'I don't think it's something that can be answered in five minutes. But I'll have a little try. First, it's caring more for him than you do for yourself. It's knowing a warm glow when he's near—and a blankness when he's not. It's enjoying the simple pleasures of life together—a walk in the rain holdings hands is bliss with John——' she stopped at the sight of Emma's anguished expression.

'What is it?'

'What you just said. "A walk in the rain"—Robert would have scoffed at that—so would I. It was all smart restaurants, parties, being seen in the right places——'

'Look, Emma. You're doing yourself no good thinking like this, you know. Why don't you read what he has to say?' She stood up and went over to her by the window. 'We can talk about it afterwards. I'll go and make us a cup of coffee while you do so.' She squeezed Emma's arm lightly. 'Go on. It won't bite. Read it—then see how you feel,' and she went out of the room quickly.

The letter was brief, but clear. Robert apologized for the things he had said, hoped Emma would forgive him because he loved her dearly, and knew she loved him still ... and would call at the flat on Tuesday to see her and talk it over—— She looked at her watch. He might be there now, ringing the bell, wondering where she was, if she was avoiding him. She put the letter down on the window-ledge and went out to tell Judith.

They stayed up late that night talking. And when the talking was done, Emma was even more sure of one thing. Although she knew now that she had never loved Robert, she had no desire to see him hurt. It had cost him a great effort to write; she knew his pride. The least she could do was to write back and tell him the truth. He was an attractive man, he would soon find someone else . . .

The letter was more difficult to write than she imagined it would be. But she had to do it, and when it was finished, and she sealed the envelope up, she felt a sense of relief.

Judith, watching her, ostensibly reading a book, looked across and smiled.

'That better?' she enquired.

'Yes. It's funny, I never imagined I'd have to write this kind of letter. But now I have, it's like an episode in my life is finished.'

'Quite sure?'

'Yes. Quite sure.' Her voice was decisive.

'Then can we please go to bed? I'm nearly dropping.'

'Oh, Judith! I'm so sorry——' Emma was all contrition immediately, and her friend laughed.

'Hey, it's not *that* bad—but this air does something to you. I'm sure I shall sleep like a log.'

'Everything's ready for you. Come on up and we'll just check.'

Emma was tired too. The letter had taken more out of her than she would have thought. But even so, she lay awake for quite a while, watching the curtains blowing gently in a slight breeze. She was getting used to the lightness at night, the 'simmer dim', as Miss Murray had told her. She said the words softly to herself, liking them, liking a lot of things about this place, unlike anywhere she had

68

ever been to before. It was so remote, so far from her usual life that she could feel changes within herself already. She couldn't explain what they were. She didn't want to try, for the moment she was content. Then like a picture that refused to be banished, she had an image of Greg Halcro. Not as she had last seen him at Mrs. Stevenson's cottage, but as he had been in the moments of their first meeting, by the Land-Rover on the way to Craig House. The devastating impact he had made would never be forgotten by Emma. So big, ruggedly handsome—no use for her to deny it even to herself—and with that instant force of startling hostility that had so quickly sent sparks flying between them. No use to deny that either. It was there, all the time, even when they were being comparatively civil with each other; a thread, an undercurrent of tension that never went away, an *awareness*. That was it. She turned restlessly in bed. Sleep seemed to have slipped away for the moment, and Emma sat up. Damn the man! Was he never to leave her in peace, even in her bed? She punched her pillows resentfully. No doubt he was sleeping peacefully by now—unless of course he was out again on an overnight fishing expedition.

A faint, almost unheard sound; a door closing very quietly. Heart beating fast, she ran to the window, knowing who she would see. He walked past very quickly, his boots making no sound on the hard ground, dressed in dark clothes, the moon glinting on his hair. He carried binoculars —or a camera—Emma could not be sure. Very cautiously she leaned out, hoping he wouldn't look back, or up. He didn't. Wherever he was going, and it looked as if it was towards his boat, he was going speedily, as if there was no time to lose. Emma stood back in the room, and waited, listening for the noise of the engine to start. Then she heard it, very faintly—then it was gone.

The moon was high, the breeze slight, the island slept.

All was quiet again. If she hadn't seen him, it could have all been her imagination. A picture of his boat came to her—a sleek large vessel, very clean, swift-looking. An overwhelming curiosity overcame Emma—and the beginning of an idea, so very intangible that she couldn't even put it into words. But disturbing. So much so that she knew she would not be able to sleep for a while now. Feeling her way, careful not to trip over the badly placed chair, she crept towards the door, and down the stairs. A few minutes later she was sitting by the dying embers of the fire, holding tightly to a beaker of tea. The clock on the mantelpiece beat slowly and comfortingly. It had started the first moment of her beginning to wind it, as if it had been waiting for someone to come to the house, to bring it to life again. She looked at its face, moonlight glinting on the hands; nearly one in the morning—and what birds would he be able to photograph with that camera at this time of morning? They didn't like being disturbed. He of all people would have enough sense to leave them in peace at night. And you didn't need camera or binoculars to catch fish, did you?

And if I'd any sense, Emma thought wryly, I'd leave well alone and forget what I've seen, because as Judith said, there just aren't smugglers living next door—but she couldn't, she knew that. And the idea grew, and crystallized, and even though she tried, it refused to go away. Somehow, some way, and soon, Emma was going to look over Greg Halcro's boat. If he was up to no good—and that would explain his brittle hostility—she intended to see for herself.

# CHAPTER FIVE

THE idea was still there in the fresh clear light of morning. Emma stood by the cooker, timing the eggs by the second hand on her watch. She could hear Judith washing in the bathroom. In a minute she would be down, and the table was laid, bread buttered—they would have to walk to the shop later today—tea cosy over the pot of freshly brewed tea. Clouds scurried low across the sky. It would rain soon. The radio was sending pop music out to the nation, but Emma wasn't really listening. She was remembering Greg Halcro sneaking silently across the grass to his boat.

'Good morning!'

'Good morning, Judith.' Emma turned. 'Did you sleep well?'

'Like a log.' She stretched and yawned. 'Oh, that's better. I could go back for another hour, but I heard you up.'

'I was going to bring you breakfast in bed if you hadn't got up—we've got to look after you, you know.'

Judith laughed. 'Heavens, I'm not delicate, I keep telling you. What are we doing today?'

'We'll go to post our letters, and do a bit of shopping. We could call on the Misses Murray as well, if you fancy.'

'Fine.' Judith sat down at the table. 'Anything I can do?'

Emma hid a grin. 'You can pour out two cups of tea— oh! They're ready!' She whipped the pan from the gas and lifted the eggs out with a spoon into eggcups.

She waited until they were half way through breakfast before she spoke again. 'I saw Greg Halcro going out last

71

night,' she said.

Judith looked up from her task of transferring the second boiled egg into the cup. 'Oh! Where to?'

'His boat.'

Judith shook her head faintly. 'I don't see——' she began.

'Well, do you need binoculars or camera for fishing?' Emma demanded.

'Was he carrying them?'

'One or the other—I couldn't see which.'

'Oh, Emma, does it matter? I mean, there's nothing wrong in taking binoculars out with you—especially up here, it's practically light all the time. I don't see anything sinister in it——' and then she paused, and a certain look came into her eyes, 'Emma, what *is* it?'

'Well, I do. I'm going to look over his boat.'

'What!' The egg nearly flew out of its cup as Judith's hand jerked. 'Oh, Emma, leave well alone——'

Emma shook her head obstinately. 'I want to know why he's so keen for me—us—not to be here—and he is, you can't deny that. He might have been reasonably civilized yesterday at that old lady's house—but don't be fooled by it—I don't trust him at all.'

'No,' Judith agreed thoughtfully. 'I know you don't— and there is something about him—but look, we're on holiday. Whatever he's doing, and I'm sure he's no crook, it's none of our business. He can't force us to go. I doubt if he's going to set the dogs on us—so——' and she grinned impishly, 'why don't you concentrate on looking after your delicate friend instead?'

'You're so practical, aren't you?' Emma sighed. 'The best way to be, I suppose—but still——' and she shrugged. The subject of Greg Halcro was dropped, but her determination remained.

72

When they set out to go to the village an hour or so later, his two dogs were scampering round, playing outside. So he was home again. Emma's head went irresistibly round to look at the cottage, an impulse she immediately regretted— because he was standing in the doorway watching them. He gave a mocking salute, and Emma nodded, then turned quickly back. There was a blustery wind blowing and both girls wore macs, Emma's a gay red with matching hat, Judith's dark blue, a headscarf over her dark reddish curls. Occasional drops of moisture touched their cheeks, but the rain had not actually started. Emma thought how lovely it would be, after their long walk, to curl up on a chair by a warm glowing fire, and drink coffee. And that was something that had never appealed before. It made her say quite suddenly to Judith: 'You know, I think I'm beginning to appreciate the simple things in life now,' and she told her why.

'I know exactly what you mean!' was Judith's delighted rejoinder. 'And listen to the radio,' she added.

'And know there's a lovely casserole waiting in the oven——'

'The tantalizing aroma drifting in from the kitchen——'

'Stop,' Emma begged, 'or I'll go back right now. We'll never make it.' The letter to Robert was in her bag. It had to be posted today, before she regretted writing it.

'What was he doing?'

'Oh! You saw him? Just standing in the doorway watching the dogs.'

'Or us,' said Judith.

'Or us,' agreed Emma drily. 'He probably thinks we'll scare his precious birds in this clobber. And I'm carrying this stick, like an idiot. I'm sure he was having us on, just another of his little ploys to make us feel unwanted.'

'Hmm, then why don't you ask the old ladies, or Mr

Grant, when we visit them?'

'A good idea. We'll do that.'

Which they did, when they at last reached the village. Mr. Grant appeared delighted to see them and insisted on taking them in the back of the shop to meet his wife. He confirmed Greg Halcro's advice about carrying a stick, and added that it was usually only if they ventured too near to the birds' nesting grounds that the attacks happened.

Then Emma remembered something else, and asked if there were any children on Skeila.

He shook his head. 'Ah now, it is sad but true. All the young people are gone and no more come. The school has been closed for several years, is it now, Annie?'

His small white-haired wife popped her head in from the kitchen. 'Ten years it is. There are only the old ones left, pensioners mainly. A shame, but there it is.'

'There is nothing here for young ones. Knitting is one big industry in Lerwick, but even there it is difficult to get young girls to train for it. They are attracted by other jobs with more money—and so it is the older ones who carry on the craft. Show them some of the things you've made, Annie.'

They were both astounded, thinking to see a few jumpers, when Mrs. Grant produced several beautifully knitted, brightly patterned cardigans, and then, from the sideboard in the corner of the living room, a cardboard box. She lifted a layer of tissue paper out, then, very carefully, a delicate lacy stole. Emma gasped, Judith leaned forward and said: 'May I hold it?'

'Of course.' The old woman smiled as Judith lifted the cobwebby, cream-coloured stole and touched it.

'Why, it's simply lovely,' she said softly.

'Ah, it's nothing,' but the old lady's face glowed with pride as she said it.

74

'Do you sell them?' Emma asked.

'Oh yes. A shop in Lerwick buys all I make.'

'Could I buy something?' Judith asked.

'If you like. Come upstairs, I'll show you both some more things.'

'And I'll go and make up your order,' said Mr. Grant, 'for I feel as if I'm not wanted here, with you ladies talking about knitwear.'

The next hour passed quickly. And when at last the girls left the shop, Emma was the possessor of an off-white Shetland cardigan which she knew would look perfect over her slim-fitting black trews. Judith carried the stole with which she had fallen in love. Both were delighted with their purchases.

'And I thought this would be one holiday where I wouldn't spend much money,' Judith said, when they were at last on the way homewards, after spending some time at the old ladies' house as well. 'I can see me going back there for more before we leave.'

'Me too,' Emma agreed. 'They'd go down well in London. The girls would go mad to get their hands on sweaters like those——' and she stopped suddenly as she realized, with a sense of shock, that she had given no thought to her modelling, or all her friends in that busy world, for a few days. She went on hurriedly, for Judith was sometimes too astute, 'I must get a few postcards and send them off next time we go shopping.'

'Mm, yes, so must I. You tend to forget everything up here, don't you?'

Emma looked quickly at Judith, but her face was very innocent.

'Oh, look at that!' London was forgotten again as Emma pointed at the bird which swooped across in front of them and vanished over the crest of the hill. Like a gull only

75

thinner, it had a pointed beak.

'I wonder what it was?' said Judith. 'Now there's an idea!'

'What?' Emma changed hands with her shopping bag. It seemed less heavy that way. Oh, for a car!

'Well, *he's* supposed to be writing a book on birds—only *you* don't think so—and we keep seeing all these strange-looking ones that we don't recognize. What is more natural than to ask him if he has a book of photos that we can borrow?'

'Well——' Emma's mouth curved into a smile. 'Good thinking, Judith. And wouldn't it be strange if he hadn't one?'

'Very strange,' agreed her friend drily. 'I think you'll find he will have. We'll ask him when we get back. You never know——'

'Never know what?'

'Oh, nothing!' was the airy reply. 'I was just going to add that it might make him seem more human if we got him talking on his subject. Then I thought I wouldn't bother.' She yawned. 'Oh, for that cup of coff—— oh, damn it!' This as the rain cascaded down with a sudden force that took them by surprise.

They began to walk faster, laughing as the huge drops bounced up from the narrow road, blinded as the rain coursed down their faces and necks. And all Judith could think of was her stole as she moaned: 'Oh, I hope it's well wrapped up!'

'You should have worn it under your mac,' was Emma's unsympathetic retort. They were running now, and the world was a grey-silver blur around them, and laughter filled the air as they made their way home, and Emma wondered why she should feel happy when she was getting soaked.

The houses came into view, mistily through the rain, and they were a welcome sight, a haven. But they didn't know of the shock which awaited them.

The key turned easily in the lock and with huge sighs of relief the girls went in, shaking the drops from their coats, putting the shopping bags down, and then——

'Oh, Judith, *look*!' Disbelieving horror in her voice made Judith turn, and see what Emma was looking at. Soot piled up in the hearth, spilling out over the rug, and everything in the room was coated with a black powder.

Emma shut her eyes, the mood of inexplicable happiness shattered into thousands of tiny fragments as she heard Judith's shocked exclamation.

'What on earth can have happened?'

And then there came a knock at the door. Judith turned because she was the nearer, and opened it, and Greg Halcro came in. There was soot on his hands and face, and Emma seeing him burst out: 'What have you done?'

For a brief moment, anger was in his eyes, then was gone. 'What do you mean?' he answered. 'Do you think *I* did this?' Faint irony coloured his words.

'You're covered in soot,' she said, but she faltered. 'And how did you know?'

'Because it's happened to me,' he retorted evenly, 'and because I warned you about your chimney when you came —but you wouldn't listen. So I came to check——' and he shrugged. 'However, if I'm not wanted——'

'Please,' said Judith, her smile warm. Judith the peace-maker. 'Please don't go. It was a terrible shock to us when we got in and saw this, as you can imagine. Surely we can go out into the kitchen and make that cup of coffee——' this with a slight, warning glance at Emma, 'and decide how best to clear the mess up.' She turned again to Greg.

77

'Perhaps you can help us on that, Mr. Halcro.'

He nodded. His eyes went to Emma. They were a very cold grey, she thought. 'If that's all right with *you*, Miss Laing?' He was waiting. If she dared to answer him rudely he would just walk out, she knew. She swallowed her pride.

'Please have a cup of coffee with us,' she said. 'I'm sorry I spoke so sharply to you—I felt very shocked.'

'I'm sure you did,' he answered. 'As I did when it happened to me. There was a heavy gust of wind downwards, and this, together with the rain, did the trick.' He followed Emma out to the kitchen. She felt his presence behind her, and it was odd, but she sensed that he wasn't displeased by what had happened. But there was nothing she could do about it. He was aggressive enough at the best of times. She shuddered inwardly at the thought of rousing his anger as well. He would have a formidable temper, she imagined. She was suddenly glad of Judith's soothing presence. And Judith was taking charge, filling the kettle, lighting the gas, putting the cups out on the table, winking at Emma when Greg crossed to the window to look out.

Emma gave her a faint smile back, as if to reassure her. The smell of soot was everywhere, even though there was none in the kitchen, which was a relief. Outside the rain thudded relentlessly down. And Greg said: 'Where's your brush and shovel?'

'Oh. In the cupboard.' Emma went quickly to the broom closet by the side of the back door.

'I'll get the worst up now and take it outside.' He reached past Emma for the old mac which hung inside the cupboard and their bodies touched briefly and she moved away.

'Yes. Thank you,' she said, and she was confused, she didn't know why. She handed him the shovel and broom and followed him into the living room. He bent and lifted

78

the soot-covered hearthrug up, banged it against the kerb to loosen the dirt clinging to it, and began to sweep inwards to the fire. 'Can I help?' she asked.

'Yes. Go and get a bucket.'

'Of course.' She ran out to the kitchen. Don't keep him waiting.

'Will that do?' She handed him the red plastic rubbish bin that they kept under the sink.

'It will need a good wash after, but yes, it will do.' And he looked up at her, and it was hard to tell what there was in his eyes now. 'You've got a big smudge on your nose,' he said, and turned away again.

Emma took a deep breath. Oh, what a lovely man you are, she said inwardly. The perfect gentleman, without a doubt. 'Have I? It'll wash off, I dare say.'

'I dare say,' he agreed, without turning. He worked unhurriedly, so as not to spread it further. The rug looked as if it would need a good shake at the very least.

He filled the bucket with soot and stood up. 'I'll empty this behind the coalshed,' he said. 'One more lot should do it. Then we'll get your fire lit again.'

'Thank you.' She watched him walk out to the kitchen, put the mac over his head and go out. He came back and finished the sweeping, looked at Emma.

'A cloth?' he suggested. 'Damp, with a touch of washing-up liquid on?' The voice was mocking, implying that she might have thought of it herself. Emma felt herself go pink.

'Yes. At once.' She ran out again and muttered a few unladylike swear-words under her breath as she rummaged under the sink for the floor-cloth—and looked up to see Judith was fighting back laughter.

'You look gorgeous,' she whispered, voice trembling.

'Thanks, I already know. *He* told me,' Emma answered.

She didn't know why, but she was beginning to feel very irritable with the big, helpful-unhelpful man in the next room. He was utterly maddening without apparently making an effort to be so. And he had kissed her. For some reason she had forgotten all about that incident. She squeezed the cloth out under the tap, poured some green washing-up liquid in the centre, and walked quickly back.

He was waiting. Patiently. Just standing there. 'Ah, at last,' he said.

'*I* can do it. Really,' she said. 'You've done enough.'

'Fine.' And he walked out with the second bucketful of soot, and the rolled-up rug under his arm. Emma knelt by the fireplace and began the careful cleaning up. Already things were looking better. The carpet would need a going over with the sweeper, of course, and everything would need a good dust, but the first depressing reaction had gone. Instead she began to feel an unwilling gratitude towards Greg Halcro. And the coffee would be even more enjoyable, if only to remove the dry acrid taste of soot that clung in the air. On impulse Emma went and unfastened the window catches and flung them wide open. Already the rain was stopping and a distant sun peered hopefully through the clouds, catching floating particles of soot in its gleam, turning them to glittering black.

The fireplace was stone, and already it shone again after one wiping over. She picked up the cloth and took it out to the kitchen to rinse out and repeat the task. Greg was washing his hands and face at the sink. Judith waited with a towel. 'Thanks.' He rubbed his face vigorously, then his hands. 'Want to come here?' he asked, and moved aside for Emma.

'The coffee's ready,' Judith said, as if determined not to give anyone an opportunity to argue.

'I'll just wipe the fireplace over again, then I'll be out,'

Emma told her. When she had finished that, and went out, both Greg and Judith were sitting at the table drinking coffee. Emma picked hers up and took a good swallow.

'Lovely!' she sighed. 'It won't take long now.' She remembered her manners. 'Was your room bad, Mr. Halcro?'

'Greg,' he said. 'The name's Greg——'

'It seems too silly being formal when we're next-door neighbours,' Judith cut in quickly. Emma had heard them talking while she had been busy. Judith was wasting no time. She looked at her friend, whose face was brightly innocent.

'Greg,' she said. It was an effort. 'Was it?'

'Not as bad as this,' he answered.

'Well, this chimney has certainly had a good clean out, I would think,' said Emma. 'I mean, judging by the amount that came down it.' She was not going to be rude to him, or rise to any baits. She would make Judith proud of her, she *would*. Even if it was an effort.

'Maybe you're right. We'll see.' And he smiled at her. His face was different when he did that, utterly different. Perhaps he could be nice when he wanted to be.

'It's been very kind of you to offer to help us,' Emma said. 'The room really doesn't look bad at all now. It'll soon be clean.'

'It will. Well——' he glanced at his watch, 'I'd best be off. I'm sure you want to get on with it. And I have work to do.'

'Oh yes,' said Judith, as if just remembering, 'we've seen several different birds while we've been here. We wondered if you had a book we might borrow, with photos in, so that we could identify them.'

He looked thoughtful. 'I've got several. I'll look one out for you.' He stood up. 'I'll drop it in later. If you're out, I'll leave it on the shelf in the porch.'

81

'We'll take good care of it.' Judith assured him.

'I'm sure you will. Goodbye for now.' Emma followed him, to let him out. He opened the front door, half turned and looked at her. 'Don't forget to wipe that soot off your face,' he said, then added softly, 'Emma.'

She closed the door after him. For a moment she stood there, feeling very confused. Then she went back into the kitchen.

They heard him go out with the dogs later on that afternoon. And a few minutes later the roar of the boat's powerful motors started, and they saw it zoom away across the water, leaving a white trail of spray in its wake. Judith and Emma were hanging out clothes at the back of the house, and he had gone past the front, and not seen them. They looked at each other.

'I wonder where he's going?' Emma murmured.

'I wonder. What a super boat!'

'And he's taken the dogs.'

Judith laughed. 'Why not? For heaven's sake, don't make a mystery out of *that*!'

Emma smiled reluctantly. 'I'm not, but—well, the more I see of him, the less I understand him.'

'He might be saying the same of us!'

'Mmm. I wonder if he's left that book in the porch. I'll go and see.' She put down her sweater in the bowl on the ground and walked quickly round to the front of the house. The porch was empty. Perhaps he had forgotten.

'Well? Is it there?' Judith asked.

Emma shook her head. 'No.'

'He'll put it in later.'

'Yes, I dare say.' But something was nagging at Emma's mind. She didn't know what it was—yet. But she had a feeling she would.

They stayed in for the rest of the day, ironed those clothes which needed pressing when all was dry. Things didn't take long in the sharp constant breeze, and there was a certain satisfaction in seeing them clean and smooth again. The iron, a heavy ancient instrument, needed heating by the fire before use, and both girls sighed for electricity. Even so, their task was not too arduous, and as Judith succinctly put it: 'Think how we'll appreciate things like washers and electric irons when we get back!'

'I never thought this domestic lark could be fun,' agreed Emma. 'It's never appealed before—but you know something? I'm enjoying it!'

'Well, don't get carried away,' her friend warned her, 'it's the novelty of staying in a tiny cottage that appeals to you.'

'I suppose so.' Emma nodded. 'Of course you're right. But I've made up my mind to get away here more often in future. I've never felt so full of beans for ages.'

'And your next-door neighbour wouldn't have anything to do with it, I don't suppose?'

'*Him!*' Emma looked quickly at her. 'Are you joking?'

'Well, you said you were full of beans. And he seems to have a certain stimulating effect on you, love.'

'Only because he keeps me on my toes, waiting for the next barbed insult!' retorted Emma, her eyes sparkling.

Judith looked at her. 'That's what I mean! Life's not dull with him around, is it?'

'Dull? No. I've never met a man who can——' and she stopped.

'Yes? Who can what?'

'Oh, nothing.'

'Oh, come on! You can't leave it like that!'

Emma shrugged. She was pressing a skirt at that moment, the one she had travelled in, and been splashed. She paused, iron held in mid-air. 'Well, who can get me *mad* so quickly. Just with one of his looks.'

'Hm, he's never given me one, I must admit,' Judith said impishly.

'Not *that* sort of look. Not wolfish. Not *him*. I mean a cool grey stare, the sort that seems to say he knows something you don't, and he's reading your thoughts——' she stopped. 'Oh hell, I'm getting all confused!'

'You mean you're annoyed because he *doesn't* give you the old leer?'

'I didn't mean that!' Emma said hastily. 'I don't care if he's a woman-hater——'

'I wonder why he kissed you, then?'

Emma gave Judith a long, old-fashioned look. 'If you mention that again, I'll——' she brandished the iron in a mock threatening gesture, and Judith laughed.

'Sorry, sorry. Just my little joke. You shouldn't have mentioned it if it upset you so much—though mind, I'd have been annoyed if you hadn't.'

Emma sighed. 'Oh, it didn't upset me. I got over that kind of outraged feeling a few years ago. I was just annoyed. The impertinence of the man! That was what got me—and that's *all*,' she added severely.

'I believe you. Honest.' But Judith got up all the same and went to the sink to fill the kettle, and Emma couldn't see her expression.

Later on they sat in the front room and listened to a play on the radio. They planned to take a picnic lunch out the following day and explore more of the island. Mr. Grant had told them that there was an old castle a few miles past Mrs. Stevenson's house, and it afforded a fantastic view of other islands. He had given them a small map of Skeila, asked if they had binoculars, and been assured by Emma

84

that there was a pair at Craig House. 'Then take them with you,' he had said. 'I'm never out without mine.'

They talked over their proposed day out after the play had finished. 'We'll take our macs,' Emma decided. 'Even if it doesn't rain we can sit on them.'

'Macs, food, flask of tea, binoculars,' said Judith.

'Hmm, what else can we take?'

'I think that's enough, don't you?'

'Pity we've no camera——' and they heard footsteps outside, as she said it, and she paused. They listened. The footsteps stopped, then went on, and a few moments later Greg Halcro's door slammed shut.

Emma went to her own door and opened it. She knew what she would find. A book was on the shelf in the porch. She carried it in. 'That's why he stopped,' she said. 'To put this in the porch.' It was a book on birds, with a photograph of two gulls in flight on the cover. A piece of paper stuck up from the centre and she opened it curiously to see the chapter heading: 'Birds of the Shetlands.'

Judith got up from her chair and peered over Emma's shoulder. 'Hey, he did remember,' she said.

'Yes. He must have had this with him on the boat,' Emma answered. 'He sounded as if he was returning from it.' And the nagging idea came back again, the one that had troubled her before. After their tea, while Judith had been upstairs washing, she had gone to the front of the cottage and walked to Greg's house, not knowing why, driven by an impulse she didn't fully understand. And if he came and caught her she was going to say that she was just going to peep in his window and check that no more soot had fallen, for it had remained windy. But he hadn't, and she had hesitated by his porch, and then quickly, almost furtively, tried his door. It was locked—and why not? He was out. She had glanced at the lock—a brand new one, a double

85

lock. She had turned away then and gone back home, and not mentioned it to Judith, for what was there to say? 'I was being nosey, but I don't know why.'

'It looks a good one—bags of photographs. We can add that to our little list of equipment tomorrow,' Judith's voice interrupted her thoughts, and Emma handed her the book with a smile.

'Good idea. Have a look at it. I'll go and make supper. Will toast do you with your coffee?'

'Lovely. Thanks.' Judith settled down to read and Emma went out to the kitchen. She looked out of the window as she stood at the sink, but she didn't see the hills rising away from the back of the house, she saw a sleek boat named *Maria.* He had been out on it for many hours. He wouldn't be going out again, he'd be going to bed soon. There would be no need to mention anything to Judith and risk upsetting her, and she would only be away for fifteen minutes, long enough to look round it and satisfy herself, then come home to bed.

Emma made the coffee, watched the toast carefully because it had a trick of burning if you glanced away even for a moment, and the sooner they were in bed and Judith asleep, the better. No one would know, no harm would be done. She would disturb nothing. Emma wasn't sure what she would do if she found anything incriminating on board the boat. In a way she was hoping for reassurance. It seemed ages before she heard Judith's steady breathing from the other bedroom. Heart beating rapidly, she got up out of bed and pulled on the dark trousers and sweater she had left ready. The wellingtons were downstairs in the broom cupboard. She wasn't sure if she would have to wade through water to reach the boat. Quietly, quickly down the stairs, wellingtons on, front door open, the catch up so she wouldn't need to fumble with a key on her return, and then

86

she closed it very quietly behind her. There was no going back now. Walking carefully across the slightly boggy ground, still damp from the rain, Emma made her way to Greg Halcro's boat.

# CHAPTER SIX

IT looked so peaceful and beautiful at its mooring that for a moment she hesitated. Was she being utterly foolish? Worse, was she being criminal? It was trespass, no doubt about that, and if she should accidentally damage anything...

But she wouldn't, and she would only be a minute anyway, and if he hadn't been so utterly hostile, she wouldn't have bothered, so it was *his* fault...

Emma scrambled up the ladder at the side and over on to the deck. Silence all around, the boat gently moving, a faint creak the only sound to be heard.

Emma walked carefully along the deck, down the steps to the cabin, pushed open the door and went in. For a second she stood there to accustom herself to her surroundings. The light from outside was enough to see everything, but it was all colourless, shadowy for the moment. Gradually things grew clearer, and she saw the two bunks, the neat cupboards, nothing out of place. A wave of dismay swept over her as she realized precisely what she was doing. But she was here. To leave now would be cowardice. She bent and slipped off the wellingtons and put them neatly to one side. In stockinged feet she walked forward and tried the small door at the end of the cabin. It opened to reveal a tiny galley with sink, gas ring on gimbals, more cupboards— very innocent-looking, all clean and gleaming. With a sigh Emma bent and opened the first cupboard. Rows of tinned food looked back at her. She shut that and opened the next.

Plates and beakers were slotted in wooden slats, all secure from breakage. Emma bit her lip. What had she hoped to find? Bottles of illicit whisky? Drugs? Whatever it was, it wasn't here. She turned round to see the cupboard over the door and reached up, and the boat rocked, and footsteps came overhead and she froze in utter terror. For a moment she literally couldn't move, so frightened was she. He'd come back!

Her heart hammered violently and her palms were clammy, her whole body trembling with the shock of imminent discovery. Oh, why had she done it? Why wasn't she safe in bed right now? She looked along the cabin and saw her wellingtons. If he should come down ... She darted out, expecting to hear that deep accusing voice any second ... back to the galley, trembling like a leaf, shaking, fearful and hiding behind the door, praying that he would go away again, have only come back for some forgotten item ...

Then the engine throbbed, and became a roar that filled the boat, and shook the galley, and somewhere in a cupboard one tin was too close to another so that it rattled slightly, insistently, and the boat began to move, and the rattling stopped. Emma turned looking desperately for a means of escape—a porthole—and saw the white-faced vision staring back at her from the mirror and looked quickly away again.

Her brain was functioning again after the few moments of panic. She had no choice but to remain where she was, for there was nowhere else to hide. And so she stood there, slipped the wellingtons on again—and waited. But where was he going? And why? And suddenly she didn't want to know. She didn't want to discover whether he was a criminal or not, she just wanted to be at home, at Craig House, tucked up in a warm bed with the prospect of a picnic the following day, and nothing more to worry about than whether or not it would rain ...

It seemed an eternity of waiting. She could see the sky outside the tiny portholes, and she didn't know how fast they were going, or where to, and then, suddenly, the engines cut out, and there was a gentle swell, and a drifting movement, and Emma's mouth was dry with fear as she stood there holding fast to a cupboard, feeling faintly sick.

Then footsteps, coming down, the cabin door opening. Silence. The hairs at the back of her neck prickled, and Emma trembled.

'Well, well, what a surprise! And what are you doing here?' Greg Halcro faced her, big, angry, tough. 'As if I didn't know. Spying, eh? Like you were today when you tried my door. Did you think it would be unlocked?'

'H-how did you know?' Absurd how you could seize on some trivial point like that.

'Never mind. I did. And now this. Does Judith know where you are?' he demanded.

Emma shook her head. 'No. She's asleep.'

The light and shadow lent a sinister darkness to his features, a piratical expression. Emma was afraid of him now, for he stood there before her, one arm on the door, blocking any chance of escape. Suddenly he moved back into the cabin. 'Come and sit down,' he said.

Emma obeyed. It was the only thing to do. He sat on the opposite bunk. 'Okay, let's hear it.'

She looked at him. The worst had happened. She had been discovered. 'I just wanted to s-see round your boat,' she said.

Greg laughed. 'Oh, come on, you can do better than that, surely? See round my boat? At midnight?'

Emma stood up. 'I'm not staying *here*,' she said. 'I'm going.'

'Where to? Know where we are? The middle of the sea.

So what are you going to do—swim?'

'W-why have you stopped here?'

'Because I knew damn well you were aboard, and I wanted to find out why where you couldn't run off. And here, you can't. In fact, not to put too fine a point on it, you're my prisoner!' And he reached across and took her arm and pulled her down again. 'So sit down. You're stopping there until you've told me what you're up to.'

'I don't have to tell you anything.' She rubbed her arm where his fingers had held it. 'And I want to go home.'

'Home? To London?' He was mocking her.

'To Craig House.'

'You call that home?'

'It is for the moment. Yes.' Her courage was returning. He seemed angry, but not violently so. And he didn't seem at all surprised at her presence. If she kept her head, she would be all right—she hoped. She crossed her fingers in childish superstition and tilted her chin in sudden defiance. 'All right, so I'm your prisoner. What are you going to do?'

He pursed his lips. 'Hmm. I'll have to think, won't I? Feed you to the sharks? Make you walk the plank?'

'You're not funny,' she snapped, and looked away.

'Then how does the thought of spending the rest of the night with me amuse you?' he said, his mouth twisting in a cynical smile.

'It doesn't either. I'm not frightened of *you*. I can look after myself.'

'You can't even stop me kissing you,' he rejoined swiftly. 'Or have you forgotten?'

Emma hesitated for only a second. 'That?' She laughed. 'Heavens, was I supposed to remember?'

'Then let's see how this grabs you,' and he leaned over and put his arms roughly round her, and kissed her. Dark, deep, effortless, because he was so strong, and she was helpless to resist—in more ways than one, although she didn't have time or wits to think why, at that moment. Not until later did she realize.

'Get *off* me!' She was shaking when the kiss was over, and she pushed him away angrily.

'You've let me down, little wildcat,' he said, amused, and lifted her chin with his hand. 'Where's the fire, that temper of yours?'

She knocked his hand away. 'Try it again and you'll find out!' Her eyes sparkled, her breast heaved as she fought to calm herself.

'Don't tempt me. I might find out more if you get in a real temper. You might tell me the truth then——'

'There's nothing to tell,' she breathed hard. 'I was curious——'

'So you came snooping round to check up on me. What do you expect to find here? Guns? The proceeds of some bank robbery? Go ahead, search the boat. Search me if you want.' He held up his hands. 'Although I won't promise not to laugh. I'm very ticklish——'

'I wouldn't *touch* you,' she retorted.

He grinned wolfishly. 'Pity—I'd enjoy that. Well, go on. Off you go—search it.'

'No. I want to go back to Skeila.'

'Hard luck, honey. You'll have to wait until I'm ready to take you. And I'm not—yet.'

'Where—where are you going?' She couldn't keep the tremor out of her voice.

He laughed. 'Scared? That's good. It might teach you a lesson.'

'You can't do anything to me——'

'No? Judith doesn't know where you are, you told me so yourself——'

'I left her a note. She'll find it when she wakes up——'

'Liar! You don't even sound convincing, let alone look it. You must do better than that, little girl, if you want to grow up to be a spy——'

'Shut up!' Emma put her hands to her ears. 'Leave me alone!'

He reached across to pull her hands away, then jerked her to her feet, and stood up himself. 'Now,' he said, 'what are you going to do? You can't move. So don't tell me to shut up, and don't try to fight me, because I'm a good deal stronger than you. Just listen.' And he shook her wrists gently. '*Why* are you on *my* boat at night?'

For a moment Emma glared helplessly at him. It was no use. She might as well tell him. She couldn't be any worse off if she told the truth.

'Because I think you're either a criminal or a smuggler,' she said. 'You made it quite clear when I came that you wanted me to go away again—and everything you've done since has only confirmed that. I don't know why you dislike me so much. I'd done nothing to you—and you're always going out at night—and I don't think you're really writing a book at all——' and she stopped, because she was saying too much, and she didn't like the look on his face.

He gave a grim smile. 'That's interesting. Why aren't I writing a book? Tell me.'

Emma bit her lip. No use to drag Mr. Grant in it. She shook her head.

'Just—instinct. Let me go, please, you're hurting my wrists.'

Slowly he released her. 'I'm not a criminal,' he said. 'I'm not on the run, and I've never smuggled anything in my life.'

Strangely enough, she believed him. But there were more things, inexplicable things, that she didn't understand. And

93

an undercurrent of tension that was oddly disturbing filled the small cabin and surrounded them. '*Are* you writing a book on birds?' she burst out.

'You doubt me? I'll show you my research and photos when—if—I ever let you go back to Skeila.' His eyebrows lifted in amusement. And mockery.

She wanted to say she didn't believe him, but she dared not. But the thought that had bothered her hours previously came back, and she said: 'Then why did you only put the book about birds in our porch *after* you'd been out in your boat?'

'Because it was here, on board *Maria*. I'd left it here a few days ago, and it's the best book for your purposes.'

It was pat, it was plausible, but she didn't believe him. Something else came back briefly to her mind, and because she thought she might just shake his poise, she went on: 'And you *knew* I was a model—and it wasn't just because I look like one, because I looked anything but chic when we first met—so how did you know?'

He laughed. 'Shrewd too. It seems I've been underestimating you. Now how *did* I know?' He frowned as if in deep thought. 'There must have been something.' He clicked his fingers. 'I know—the clothes. Very expensive-looking they were——'

'Rubbish!' Emma burst out. 'They're from a chain store——'

'Ah yes! But the way you wore them. Superb!' He kissed his encircled finger and thumb in a Gallic gesture. Emma felt as if the ground was being swept away from under her feet; as if his mockery took any edge off her anger—and it was puzzling too. Because why should he behave so? He had been angry at first. Now it seemed as if he was not. He was changing, subtly but quite definitely, and she was no longer where she was with him. Not that she had before, but at least his mood had been quite decisive then. She began to feel strangely helpless. He had an answer for everything.

'You're like a—a—politician!' she breathed hotly. 'You're somehow twisting everything I say round.' She put her hand to her head. 'You know what I'm getting at, and yet you say things until I'm not sure what I do mean.'

'Really? How utterly fascinating! You'd better sit down again. It's late.'

'I know it is. I'm tired. Please let me go home. I'm sorry I came on your boat—I'm sorry I'm staying next door—I'm sorry I ever met *you*!' she finished.

'Harsh words. Meant, no doubt, but a bit late in the day to be uttered. I mean, you are here, you are staying next door—and you *have* met me.' He gave a crooked grin. 'I said *sit down*.'

She sat down. 'And you're bossy,' she muttered.

'Oh yes, I am. As you'll find out even more certainly if you keep messing me about like this. You've ruined a perfectly good night's fishing——'

'Huh!' Emma couldn't stop the disbelieving exclamation. She felt a helpless anger sweeping through her. But she didn't know how to get the better of him. It was an experience new to her; meeting someone like Greg Halcro who was utterly unlike any man she had ever met in her life before, with whom she sensed the usual feminine wiles wouldn't work. Or would they? She glanced quickly down at her hands lest he see her face. Would tears do the trick? There was only one way to find out. But not yet—not just yet. She remembered something else. 'And they're all old people on Skeila——' it was quite a ridiculous thing to say. But somehow it seemed quite appropriate at that moment.

He looked astounded. 'So? That's not my fault. I've not killed off all the younger set.'

'I didn't mean *that*.' She wasn't sure what she did mean at the moment. 'But why are *you* here?'

'Why not? It's quiet—or it was before *you* came——'

'I don't like you!' she blurted out.

'I know that!'

'And I know you don't like me,' she added.

'And does that bother you?' his tone was oddly gentle, for him.

'Of course not!'

He began to laugh. 'You're a funny girl, you know that?'

'I'm not!' Emma was beginning to feel angry. 'Don't say that.'

'Funny girl,' he repeated it with relish. Emma stood up and brushed past him, and ran up the steps to the deck. She wasn't sure where she was going, but she knew if she stayed in the cabin a moment longer with him she would undoubtedly do something she would regret.

She stood by the rail of the boat and looked out to sea. A grey mist hung low over the water to her right, and there could have been land there, she wasn't sure. Nothing was familiar; there was an eerie strangeness about everything that could be frightening. She shivered, suddenly cold and sad. What was she doing here anyway? What was she doing staying in this remote spot for a holiday, where everything was completely alien to her normal way of life? There was no one to answer.

He came up behind her. 'Get below,' he said. 'It's cold up here.'

'No, I won't,' she said, and put her hands on the rail.

'Yes, you will. And you'll stay there too.'

'Not with *you* I won't.' She kept her back to him.

'I didn't say with me. I'm going to start the boat in a minute, and I want to know where you are——'

'You're not locking me up in it!' She whirled round,

dismay on her face.

'Aren't I? You'll see whether I am. We're going a short trip—then, if you behave, I'll take you back to Skeila——'

It was a bad dream. It must be. She would never do anything so utterly foolish again. But she was *not* going to let herself be locked in a cabin. 'No,' she repeated. 'Start it up if you like, but I'm staying here——'

'Emma,' he said it slowly, almost resignedly, and it was odd, his use of her name, 'you wouldn't like me to take you down there by force, would you?'

Behind her, the rail was a comforting solid wall. She put her hands on it, and held it tightly—*very* tightly. She had to swallow before she spoke this time. 'You wouldn't dare,' she said.

'I would. And don't think you can resist me, because you can't. I'm much stronger than you——'

'I'll scream——'

'And nothing will happen. There's no one to hear you for miles——' He put out a hand to touch her arm. 'Come on, there's a good girl. We're wasting time standing here arguing. The sooner you go, the sooner you can be back in your own bed——'

Emma pushed his hand away and twisted herself sideways and started to run away from him. But she was confused and tired. She bumped into the rail, felt his hands on her and in a last desperate attempt to elude him, leant backwards and kicked out at him. His hands were strong, but she was agile, and twisted—and then felt the terrifying rush of space as her body tipped backwards, as she fell outwards helplessly, carried down with sudden frightening force. The sea was cold and rough, she went under with an icy rush, a dazzling star-ridden whirl of bubbles and choking. And knew she was going to drown . . .

'Hold me, you little fool.' The harsh voice wrenched her

back to semi-realization, and she had the sudden image of Greg Halcro's angry face before she closed her eyes, too engrossed in the struggle to breathe to care.

'Up—that's it. All right.' He was dragging her over the side, a furiously angry man who handled her roughly so that she felt as if her body would be wrenched in two. She lay on the deck, the hard wood under her back, and turned her head feebly to the side.

'You fell overboard, you stupid idiot.' He pulled her to her feet. 'And if you say much more, so help me I'll give you a damn good hiding. Get in that cabin!'

'I don't——'

'In the bloody cabin!' As though suddenly too impatient to bother arguing further, he swung her up in his arms and carried her down the steps. 'Stand there—you don't sit down on the bunk in those sodden clothes. Get them off— I'll get you a blanket.' Every word forcefully spoken, he was not in a mood to be argued with. He opened a drawer under one bunk and lifted out two dark grey blankets. 'I'll give you two minutes to get stripped and wrap those round you. Then you can sit down.' And he turned and went out.

Emma pulled off the soaking wet trousers and sweater, then her underclothes. She wrapped one blanket round her sarong fashion, tucked it firmly in, then put the other round her shoulders. Her clothes she put on the floor in a bundle. She was loath to arouse Greg's further ire by putting them on bunk or even on the small formica-topped table at the end of one bunk.

'Are you decent?'

'Yes.' She sat down on a bunk, and he came in.

'All right. I'll make you a hot drink. And I warn you now, I'm not in the mood for any more nonsense from you. Is that clear?'

In a small voice, Emma said: 'Yes.' And she watched

him walk into the galley. Very soon he was out again, carrying a steaming beaker.

'Cocoa—very sweet. Drink it.'

'Thank you.'

He sat opposite her and lit a cigarette. 'I don't often lose my temper,' he said, 'for which you can feel relieved.'

'I'm sorry,' the apology was difficult, but it had to be made. Because just at the moment he looked unpredictable, as if he might carry out his threat to give her a good hiding.

'So you should be.' He nodded. 'Drink that up. You'll be suffering from shock next, and I don't relish carrying you back to your friend's in that condition.'

'I'm strong,' Emma said defiantly. 'I'll be all right in a minute.'

'I'm pleased to hear it. Your clothes won't. You'll have to go home in blankets. I hope you're good at explaining things.'

Her heart missed a beat. 'But—w-won't we be b-back before——'

'Before she gets up? I don't know. Is it bothering you now?'

Emma bit her lip. 'I'll be freezing before morning.'

'You should have thought of that before you made your spectacular escape bid, shouldn't you?'

'I wasn't—I mean, I didn't *intend* to go over. I was running away from you. I didn't want to be locked in——' she faltered, because there was no softness on the face watching her, only a cynical detachment. She took a long drink of the cocoa. There seemed to be no advantage to be gained from pleading. His hard face showed not a vestige of anything approaching sympathy. He would, she sensed, be quite immune to tears as well. Therefore, Emma thought, regaining her wits a little more with each swallow of the deliciously hot drink, I'll shut up and let him talk. Things can't be any worse than they are now, and he's not going to murder me, so I'll just sit here—and see what happens. She looked up at him. Perhaps something of her thoughts showed on her face.

'Lost your tongue?' he enquired softly.

'No. I'm not wasting my time talking to you. Do what you're going to and leave me alone.'

The merest glimmer of a smile touched his mouth. 'You learn fast. All right, finish your drink and we'll go.' He stood up. 'Aren't you going to ask where?'

'No.'

He began to laugh. 'That's better. I'm taking you back to Skeila—back to the bed you wish you'd never left.'

Emma put her empty beaker down on the table. 'Thank you.'

'Don't thank me. I didn't want you here anyway,' and with that he walked out of the cabin and up the steps. Emma heard the engines start, felt the deep rumble beneath her making the entire cabin throb, and she thought about Greg Halcro. She had never met anyone like him in her life—ever. She was cold, and she pulled the blankets tighter round her.

There was a slowing down, a faltering of the engine note, then they cut out, and he called: 'Emma, come up on deck!'

She went quickly, fearing his impatience, and he was waiting for her on deck. 'Come on,' he said. 'Follow me over the side.'

The familiar cliffs loomed up through faint mist, and the boat was in shallow water. She climbed over and down the ladder and he lifted her as she reached the bottom and carried her to the beach. Then he put her down.

'Goodbye,' she said.

'Not yet. I'm seeing you safely in your house—or who

knows what else you may get up to?'

'Dressed like this?' she flashed, looking up at him.

'I wouldn't put anything past you. Anything at all,' he added softly, and took her arm. 'Come on.'

'Take your hand off me, I can walk—ouch!' She had forgotten that she was barefoot. A sharp stone reminded her, painfully, and she hopped in agony.

'It looks like it!' Was he laughing? If he was—she looked quickly up at him, but he was straight-faced again.

'Yes! As long as I watch where I'm going.' And she marched away upwards, but treading carefully now, looking, checking before each step. He was beside her, striding easily, this big infuriating man she so disliked.

Then she trod on a concealed stone, and it was agony, and she faltered, biting back an exclamation of pain, and Greg Halcro swung her up into his arms with the exasperated words: 'God save me from helpless idiotic women!'

'Oh!' Emma struggled furiously. 'Put me down at once! How dare you——'

'Shut up, woman. If you think I've got all night to waste while you fumble and stumble over rocks—I haven't. So keep quiet or I'll——'

'You hateful beast!' Emma's flailing arm landed against the side of his head with a crack and he put her roughly, abruptly to the ground and pulled her towards him. He was angry now, and making no attempt to hide it.

'Stop fighting me, you little hellcat——' She jerked her arm free and began to run away from him, towards the house. Shreds of mist swirled round her face, and the air was cold and dank. She no longer cared about her feet, she just wanted to get away from *him*. His running steps were dark and heavy after her, and if he caught her—and then he did. And the blanket fell from her shoulders to the ground as he whirled her round to face him. She clutched her

101

sarong as he grabbed her, and shook her.

'Oh, you're hurting. Let me go!'

'You want a good beating——'

'Not from *you*!' And suddenly she stopped struggling. Because if the other blanket came off...

He bent and picked up the second one and flung it at her. 'Put that on now,' he commanded, 'and think yourself lucky you're a woman and not a man.'

Emma wrapped the blanket tightly round her shoulders and turned away from him. She was too angry and upset to speak. She began walking more slowly, carefully, and tears welled unbidden in her eyes, nearly blinding her, but she was careful not to stumble or fall. She didn't want him to touch her.

The houses appeared, huddled grey shapes, still and waiting, and her heart lifted slightly. In a few minutes, it would be all right. He would have gone away again...

She pushed at the door and it opened softly, and she turned, and he pushed it wide open after her and followed her in.

'I don't——' she began, a tremor in her voice.

'I'm not staying,' he interrupted harshly. 'What the hell are you crying for?'

'I'm not—I'm not——' but she had to stop.

'For heaven's sake,' he ran impatient fingers through his hair. 'If anyone should be crying, it's *me*, with all the aggravation you've caused me.'

'You're a *beast*,' she whispered, and it was an effort to get the word out, but she managed.

'Yes, I know. And you're a nosey child who shouldn't go around meddling in other people's affairs. You're on holiday. Act like a holidaymaker, go for walks—in shoes—go paddling if you want—but keep away from *my boat*, unless you're invited.'

102

'Go *away*.' Her lips trembled. 'J-just go away.' She put her hand to her mouth. She began to shiver with cold, tiredness and something else. Something she didn't understand, a treacherous weakness that threatened to overwhelm her.

'For God's sake—I can't leave you like that. Have you no booze in—whisky—anything?'

She shook her head. 'No.'

He nodded. 'No. I needn't have asked, need I? Right, I'll go and get some. Meanwhile, get some clothes on, and I'll be back in a minute—and get a towel to dry your hair.'

She'd forgotten about that. It hung wet and straggly down her shoulders. She watched him go and was tempted to lock the door—but dared not. He would be quite capable of putting his shoulder to it and breaking the lock, the mood he was in. Emma ran upstairs.

When he returned minutes later she was in pyjamas and dressing gown, and rubbing her hair vigorously. He took one look that encompassed her from head to toe and held up a small bottle. 'Brandy,' he said. 'Where are your glasses?'

'Only cups—in the kitchen—on the draining board.'

She followed him out. He upended two cups and poured a measure in each. Then he handed her one.

'Drink it all,' he ordered.

It went down splendidly, warm as a fire, and she gasped. The effect was rapid. The tears had already dried, and she began to feel better. She lifted her chin.

'You can go now,' she said. 'Really. I'm fine. Thank you for the drink.'

He downed his own. 'Don't mention it. That's better. I needed a drink as well, you know. I'm not used to fishing girls out of the water at midnight.'

'I said I was sorry.' Some of the old fire had returned now, she stared defiantly at him.

'You shouldn't have said you were going to lock me in the cabin.'

'You shouldn't have sneaked aboard,' he pointed out with some logic.

'Are we going to spend the rest of the night going over it?' Emma put her cup down on the table and turned towards him. She was not aware of the picture she made at that moment, tall slender figure dressed in pale gold dressing gown, eyes large and luminous in the shadowy light, her hair flat and straight, enhancing the delicate contours of her finely boned face and feminine mouth. But Greg Halcro's eyes softened momentarily as he looked at her.

'You soon get back to normal, don't you?'

'I need to with you—you're a natural bully.'

They were facing each other in that shadowy room, with mist swirling softly outside, and a prickle of excitement touched Emma's spine. So many unusual situations since she had arrived on Skeila, and all connected in some way with this dark unpredictable man—this Viking. And she was even more convinced that mystery surrounded him—yet there seemed no way of beating him.

He began to laugh softly. 'I wonder what you'd say if I started calling *you* names like you do to me? You'd be very offended—yet I'm supposed to accept them——'

'I can't see anything upsetting you,' she shot back quickly, 'a brute like *you*——'

'Brute? What makes you say that?' He seemed genuinely interested and she half turned away. She was foolishly getting involved in an argument again, something she had resolved to avoid. 'Don't turn your back on me just because you don't like being asked something,' he said, and grasped her arm lightly to turn her towards him. 'Don't start anything you're not prepared to finish.'

'I thought you were in a hurry to get back to your pre-

104

cious boat,' she answered.

'In a minute. First let's hear why I'm a brute. Do I go around beating up old ladies or something?'

'Don't be silly—and let go of my arm.'

'That's all you ever say—let go of me—don't you like being touched?'

'Not by you.'

'It's the only way to keep you in one place.' He still hadn't taken his hand away. 'So I'm a brute, am I? And do I kiss like one?'

'I don't know—I——' She was suddenly confused, and tried to free her arm, because she knew . . .

'Then let's see if I can do it gently, shall we?' And he pulled her towards him, not at all roughly, but extremely firmly, and held her with no effort at all as he began to kiss her. Not once, or twice—she lost count, and oddly enough it didn't seem to matter because Emma was discovering with a bone-melting sensation that she had never been kissed like this before. Ever. Worse, she was actually enjoying the embrace. And as she realized that startling fact, she weakly tried to push Greg Halcro away.

'Oh no—no—stop——' she begged.

'Oh no, stop,' she mocked. 'Is that what you always say?' But already he was releasing her, as if tired of the game. She was obscurely angry and frightened of him. He had hurt her in a way she didn't understand, and she wanted to hurt him, but she didn't know how.

'Get out of my house,' she said quickly. 'Now.'

'I'm going—I've got better things to do than waste time on *you*,' he answered. 'You don't even know how to kiss properly.' And he laughed and strode out, and when he got to the door he paused. 'And I'll return your clothes in the morning,' he added. 'So you'd better get your story ready for your friend—after all, you can hardly tell her the truth

105

about your bungling little spy trip, can you?'

Emma, incensed, rushed towards him, hands upraised—but he was gone, leaving only the echo of quiet mocking laughter behind him.

# CHAPTER SEVEN

EMMA groaned and tried to push the hand away from her arm. 'Get off me, you beast,' she muttered. Why wouldn't that awful man leave her alone? Judith's laugh brought her to wakefulness.

'So I'm a beast, am I?' Her amused face swam into focus, and Emma struggled to sit up.

'Judith! It's you!'

Judith's eyebrows shot up. 'And *who* did you expect? No, don't tell me—let me guess. Er—Greg Halcro? And what precisely were you dreaming about him for?' And she sat on the end of the bed, eyes alight with delighted curiosity.

The whole sequence of memory rushed back as Emma sat there in bed, and Judith passed her a cup of coffee. 'Here, love, drink this before you talk. You look as if you've had a night out on the tiles—and what are those two blankets doing in a heap on the floor?'

'Oh, Judith!' Emma moaned it softly. 'I don't know where to begin. Something *awful* happened last night——'

'My God! *What?*'

'I wouldn't know where to start.' Emma took a swallow. Her head ached, her foot was beginning to throb, and she felt a bruise coming up on her arm where Greg had grabbed her out of the water.

'I think you'd better begin at the beginning,' her friend suggested. '*And* there's a half empty bottle of some alcohol on the kitchen table, and two empty cups—and if you can imagine what's going through my mind you'd put me out of my agony by telling me!'

Put like that, Emma could see the other girl's point of view. She began to smile slowly. 'Oh dear,' she said. 'It does sound awful—and it was—but perhaps not quite in the way you think. But it's a long story. What time is it?'

'Nearly ten. That's why I woke you—what on earth have you done to your hair?'

'Yes, well, that's part of the story. Oh, Judith! You know how I decided I'd like to see over Greg's boat——'

'Oh no, oh no——' Judith shook her head slowly. 'You didn't——'

'I did.' Emma took another swallow. 'What a fool I was...' and she began the story. It was easier to tell than she had imagined, and Judith heard her out in a silence that had a kind of amused disbelief to it, her eyes widening at each new twist and turn, her head shaking in wonderment when it was all over.

'Good grief!' was what she said when Emma had at last finished. 'What a *man*!'

'Is that all you can say?'

'For the moment, yes. I'm too startled. It'll take a while to sink in.'

'He's an absolute brute,' Emma burst out. She had missed one point out. She was not prepared to admit even to herself, let alone her friend, that she had gone weak at the knees when Greg had showed her what kissing was all about. That was something she was going to have a good talking to her subconscious mind about—but not yet, not yet.

'Hmm—well, you should know, of course.' And Judith stood up. She seemed as if about to add something else, but then she turned abruptly towards the door, as if thinking better of it. 'I'll get breakfast. You'll need food after all *that*.' And she went out.

Feeling faintly bruised and battered, Emma got out of bed to go for a wash.

Barely two hours afterwards they were setting out on their picnic. Emma's clothes blew merrily on the line at the back of the house, the sun shone again, all mists of the night blown away in the fresh sea winds, and it could have been a bad dream—except that the bundle of sodden clothing in the porch when she had opened the front door had been only too real.

Emma had washed them quickly, grimacing at the memories they evoked. And where, she wondered, was Greg Halcro? Tucked up in bed or out again on another expedition?

She closed the door behind them, put the key in her bag and caught up with the waiting Judith. 'Have we got everything? Sandwiches? Flask?' Judith asked.

'Everything. And a map. I wonder how far we'll get?'

Her friend looked at Emma amused. 'It all depends on you,' she said, 'you poor battered female. How's your foot?'

Emma pulled a face. 'I'll live. You should see the bruise on my arm where he grabbed me, though.'

'I can't wait. Still, it does have a certain romantic flavour about it, don't you think?'

Emma gave her a withering glance. 'If you weren't my dearest friend I'd begin to suspect you'd got a soft spot for that—that—*man*.'

Judith laughed. 'Now you know I'm too loyal for that. Dear me, a fellow like him? Not my cup of tea at all, dear,' but she had an amused glint in her eyes, and Emma was not completely reassured.

Greg Halcro was soon forgotten in the exhilaration of walking the springy peaty ground, making for a hill, taking it more slowly as they climbed, for Emma was mindful of Judith's condition, and worried that her friend might tire.

She knew that Judith was sensible enough to call a halt if she needed a rest, and she herself was relieved when, as they neared the top of the hill, Judith said: 'Let's sit here for a minute, shall we?'

They spread their macs on the ground and sat down. The view that surrounded them was spectacular. Misty grey islands in the distance over a sun shimmering dark sea, birds soaring high in the sky, and all about them the still quietness that was so much a part of this beautiful island, Skeila.

'I feel as if we're thousands of miles away from civilization,' Judith admitted. 'I've never been anywhere like this before—and yet I'm not sure how I'd feel about living here. It's fine for a holiday, to unwind and relax completely, but I can understand the young people leaving.'

'Yes,' Emma agreed slowly, thoughtfully. 'I know exactly what you mean—and yet——' she stopped.

'And yet?' Judith prompted.

Emma shook her head. 'I don't know. There's something —I can't explain it—it's as though there's a spell——' she looked at her friend. 'No. Forget I said it.'

Judith lifted one eyebrow. 'You talk about spells and I'm supposed to forget it. Oh come on, what sort of spell?'

Emma laughed. 'I've told you, I don't know. It's just a feeling I have, as though in a strange way, this is home— oh, you can laugh——'

'Who's laughing?' her friend said quietly. 'I dare say if John lived here, then this is just where I'd want to stay.'

Emma looked quickly at her. 'I don't see——' she began.

'No,' Judith answered, 'no, it was an odd thing to say. I don't know why I did.' She leaned forward and peered hopefully in the shopping bag. 'I'm starving,' she said, 'can we cheat and just have one little sandwich now?'

'Of course. But only one. We're going to dine in style in

that old castle.' The subject was changed. Emma was relieved, and yet, in a strange way, still slightly puzzled. Sometimes Judith came out with things that seemed so casual and unimportant—and yet—Emma shrugged and unpacked the sandwiches. Better leave it for now.

The ruins of the old castle stood on a hill overlooking the water. Nearby was another island, close enough to be reached by rowing boat, and with several long low buildings near the shore. They were too delighted with exploring the ruins in which they stood to look at the other island at first. It was only when they were sitting on a low wide wall, their picnic things spread out between them, the sun beating down on them, for they were protected from the wind, and the sun's rays were hot, that Emma looked over the water and noticed movement by the houses.

'People!' she murmured. 'Would you believe it, we're not the last people in the world after all.'

'That's a relief,' Judith was too busy spreading out the food to look. 'Oh gosh, I'll weigh a ton when I get back to London. I've never eaten so much before in my life! I'm dying of hunger now, and it doesn't seem so long ago that I was tucking into bacon and eggs.'

'I know,' Emma answered, 'it's your condition. Eating for two and all that. Still——' she tore her eyes away from the distant buildings for long enough to look at their meal. 'I'm starving too—and I've *got* to keep slim.' She wasn't really concentrating, though. There was something fascinating about that other island . . .

'Did we bring the binoculars?' she asked abruptly.

'I put them at the bottom of the bag,' and Judith pulled the case out as she said it. 'With the book on birds that seems to have caused so much trouble. If I remember rightly, we were going to do a bit of bird study today.'

'Yes.' Emma was impatient to get the binoculars out of

the leather case. 'Yes, we were—we are—but first, I just want to see that little village over there,' and she put the glasses to her eyes and stood up.

Everything sprang into sharp relief, intensely magnified, instantly, startlingly near. Only it wasn't a village. The buildings were not houses, they were wooden huts, a dozen or so of them, spread out in neat order along a line that ran parallel to the shore. There was wire fencing too. She could see it all so clearly now, yet it had been invisible before. And why had she thought they were houses?

There was a bare look about them ... Movement caught her eye, a man walking across from one hut to another, a man in overalls. He looked suddenly towards them, and Emma lowered the glasses, for it was almost as if he looked directly into her eyes. Impossible, of course. Annoyed with herself, she put the glasses to her eyes. The man had vanished. There was a very tall mast from one of the sheds. It looked like a giant television aerial.

'Judith, take a look through these,' said Emma.

'Mmm,' Judith had her mouth full. 'In a minute. What is it?'

'I don't know. It looks like a camp of some sort——' Emma stopped. A Land-Rover appeared from behind a shed and roared out, along a road to vanish in a cloud of exhaust smoke behind a hill. The sound carried clearly over the water.

'Perhaps it is.' Judith was clearly far more interested in the egg sandwich she was eating. 'I think we'll have a little cup of coffee as well. Want one?'

'Yes, please.' Some more men had appeared. Emma put the binoculars to her eyes again. There were three of them, dressed casually in dark sweaters, talking in a group. Then something very odd happened. One of the men swung binoculars to his eyes, and looked directly towards Emma

112

and Judith. For a full few seconds they were staring at one another, then Emma took the glasses down and turned to Judith, who looked up, saw her friend's face, and said: 'Goodness, what is it? You've gone white!'

'We're being spied on!' Emma gasped.

Judith began to laugh. 'What! Where?'

'Oh, don't look,' Emma moaned. 'They're watching us!'

'Well, you've been watching *them*—perhaps they're getting their own back.' And Judith stared over the water shading her eyes from the sun. 'Hmm, yes, they are. What a cheek! Quick, give me your mirror.'

'What?'

'Your mirror.' Emma, bemused, took her mirror from her bag and Judith quickly held it up, caught the sun on it— and Emma knew what she was doing, and began to laugh.

The next moment the man lifted the binoculars away from his eyes and turned away. Judith handed Emma back the mirror.

'I don't like being stared at,' she said. 'That'll teach him a lesson. He'll be dazzled for a few minutes.'

'You surprise me,' said Emma. 'I always thought you were such a quiet girl.'

'Oh, I am, I am, but I enjoy eating my lunch in peace. This is *our* place, not theirs.'

'Well, I was looking at them,' Emma felt obliged to point the matter out, just to be fair.

'Mmm, yes, you were. But they can see we're just a couple of holidaymakers, on a picnic. It's natural to look around you—they're just being nosey.' And Judith nodded firmly.

Emma grinned. She was seeing a new side to her friend. She picked up a sandwich and bit into it. 'I think I'll enjoy my lunch,' she said. 'Especially with you to look after me.'

The other laughed. 'Think nothing of it. You've got me

curious now, I must admit. I wonder what sort of place it is?'

'Mr. Grant would tell us. He knows everything—hey, let's see the map.' Emma reached over and dug it out, together with the book on birds. They spread it out on the ground, and both studied it carefully, and Emma traced a pattern across Skeila to where the ruined castle they now sat in was marked. The island they had been looking at was called Eskla, much larger than their own, stretching away in a long curved boomerang shape—but there was no mark on it to indicate what those sheds were.

And why should there be after all?

'Let's forget them,' Judith said. 'We'll spoil our picnic if we start worrying about who—and why. Ah, this is the life!' She sipped her coffee. 'I'd like to explore this place properly afterwards. I wonder if there are dungeons?'

It was too warm to talk anyway. The men had vanished, the world was silent and peaceful again, and time didn't really matter because every day was the same, and there was always tomorrow . . .

'I could go to sleep,' Judith murmured.

'Why not? We can lie on the macs. It's warm enough.' Emma put the empty sandwich bags back in the shopping bag and screwed the lid on the flask. 'Two cups left. We'll have those later.' She yawned. 'Oh, so could I.'

'Mmm, yes—well, after last night's events, I'm not surprised,' her friend told her severely. She settled herself down, and there came a distant drone of a helicopter high overhead. It flew over them, a giant mosquito with whirling wings, and vanished into the distance and a man's voice said:

'Good afternoon, ladies.' For one absurd moment Emma, kneeling down to tidy the picnic things away, thought someone had landed from the helicopter and looked up

114

startled to see a tall fair-haired man standing near them. A man dressed in dark sweater and trousers, very familiar—because he had been watching them through binoculars not so long before.

She scrambled to her feet. He was good-looking. He was also smiling, and there was nothing sinister about that smile. She felt quite guilty, squashing the emotion firmly as she answered him:

'Hello. How did you get here?'

'By boat. The view through glasses isn't really satisfactory—especially when it gets spoilt by dazzling sun's rays. So I decided to come over and say hello in person, in case you misjudged my motives.'

Judith was sitting up now. She looked at the man, smiling, because she could see the funny side of most things, and this man looked as if he could too.

'I hope I didn't give you sunstroke, Mr.——?' She paused, waiting.

'Smith. Douglas Smith, Miss——?'

'Mrs. Judith Roberts.' He was still waiting, it seemed, so she added: 'And my friend Emma Laing.'

He gave them both a slight bow. 'I'm pleased to meet you. No, I didn't get sunstroke. That was a truly professional move, Mrs. Roberts. Although, to be fair, we were only returning the compliment. You had been watching us.'

Emma smiled at him. She rather liked the look of him. He wasn't as tall or big as Greg Halcro, but he stood like a soldier, and was well built—and had a very attractive face and nice blue eyes. 'That's my fault, Mr. Smith——'

'Douglas, please.'

'Douglas. I was curious to see the houses, as I thought they were—but they're not, are they? Houses, I mean.'

'No, they're not. In fact they're very comfortable inside, but I agree the outside view isn't exactly attractive. Why

115

don't you both come back over with me? Have a look around. We're a bit short on feminine company just now.'

Emma and Judith looked at one another. A brief glance, but full of meaning, and Douglas Smith, who was apparently a great deal more astute than they gave him credit for, added: 'No strings attached, I promise you. You can stay just as long—or as short as you wish.'

Judith nodded very slightly. Emma said: 'Well, just for a little while, I'm sure you've got work to do—or are you on holiday?'

He threw back his head. He had a good hearty laugh. 'No, it's not a holiday camp, I'm afraid. We are working— but you'll see what sort of work when you arrive. Shall I carry the bag?'

Emma handed it to him. They picked up the macs and followed him down to the beach, well hidden from the castle by overhanging cliffs. There was a thin trail downwards, and both girls walked carefully, following the sure-footed man who paused half way down to ask: 'Do you want help?'

'We can manage, thanks.'

It was a small motor boat, and the reason they hadn't heard the engine, Emma realized, was because it had been drowned out by the helicopter. He helped them in, and switched on. It took only minutes for the short journey across between the two islands. The beach was very stony. It reminded Emma of her own arrival on a beach just hours previously—dressed only in a blanket. This time she was more sensibly clad in what she referred to as her Rupert Bear trousers, yellow and black check, matching yellow blouse and black flat shoes.

There was a welcoming committee to greet them, although, Emma reasoned, it must have been quite clear that Douglas was not returning alone. Four men, two middle-

116

aged, tanned and weatherbeaten, one smoking a pipe, and two younger men in their thirties, tough-looking, all casually dressed like Douglas, all very friendly and polite.

'I shall never remember your names,' Emma confessed after Douglas had introduced them all. The older pipe smoker laughed.

'We'll remind you, don't worry.' He added dryly, 'I'm Tom.' He turned to Douglas. 'I suppose it's too early to open the bar in our guests' honour?'

Douglas looked at his watch and pulled a thoughtful face. 'It all depends if you drink.' He turned to Emma and Judith. 'Do you?'

Judith smiled. 'Not usually this early,' she said. 'But please don't let it stop you.'

'Wouldn't dream of it,' Tom answered. Emma wasn't clear who seemed to be in charge. The atmosphere was very relaxed and friendly. He went on: 'You can show them round first, Doug, then they'll know what we do. I'll go and see about rustling up some food for later—you will stay for a meal, of course?' The glance was almost pleading. 'We so rarely get young lady visitors.'

Judith looked at Emma. Words weren't needed; they knew each other too well. The look said: 'They seem all right—and Tom's just like someone's dad.'

'Well,' said Emma, 'we're not in any *hurry*, but we don't want to put you out at all.'

'Not putting us out.' This was the other older man. He added helpfully: 'Malcolm.' Both girls laughed. Douglas looked at them. 'Right. Want to go a trip round the island first?'

'On foot?' queried Judith.

'By Land-Rover. The roads are narrow but good. Then I'll show you round our camp—and then the bar might well be open.'

'Sounds good,' said Emma. 'We didn't expect a conducted tour. Will we see any wildlife?'

'It all depends what you mean by wildlife,' said one of the younger men who had not yet spoken, and he added: 'I'm Philip. There are some seals round the other side—but not wild!'

'Philip is the seal man,' Tom interjected. 'We're all naturalists—or had you guessed?'

Both girls shook their heads. Naturalists! thought Emma. And Douglas grinned because something must have shown on her face. 'You thought we'd all be old men wearing glasses or something?'

'No!' she went faintly pink. 'Of course not,' but she saw that the others were grinning too and it didn't seem to matter anyway. The atmosphere was just right.

Philip came with them in a Land-Rover, and Douglas took the wheel with Emma beside him in the middle, Judith on the left, and Philip crouching in the back.

'We saw another Land-Rover before,' Emma said, as they set off. 'Is this it?'

'No. That would be Jim. You might meet him later. We've got two vehicles.'

'On the other hand,' Philip put in from his seat at the back, 'you might not. He has been known to get so engrossed in what he's doing that he forgets to return.'

And then Emma asked the question that had been at the back of her mind since they had first arrived at the camp. 'Do you know a man called Greg Halcro?' she said. 'He's my next-door neighbour, and he's writing a book on birds.'

They were bowling along the narrow track close to the sea, climbing higher, but never far away from it, always seeing it, and the island of Skeila which was rapidly being left behind them. There was *something*—she could not be sure what, afterwards when she thought about it, but a slight tense pause perhaps, and then Douglas answered.

'Greg Halcro? Big fellow. Yes, I've met him. He's got rather a nice boat, hasn't he?'

'That's the one.' Emma felt a very slight nudge from Judith by her side. The merest pressure of fingers against her arm, but it told her that she too had noticed something.

'He's your neighbour? Lucky man,' Douglas said lightly.

'I must have a word with him some time if he's writing a book about birds,' said Philip, and Emma half turned to look at him as he spoke. 'I can give him some gen—he may know something about seals too, you never know.'

'He may. He goes out fishing a lot at night, I think,' and Emma winced inwardly as she said it, remembering her own recent experience. 'He brought us a lovely fish a couple of days ago.'

'You must remind us to give you a couple to take home with you,' Douglas said. 'We practically live on fish. Still, it's supposed to feed the brain,' he grinned at them both, 'so we should stay bright.'

'Are you from a college or something?' Judith asked with interest.

From behind them Philip answered. 'No—well, not exactly. Although our work is educational in a way. We study migration in birds and sea life in these parts, it's all part of a bigger programme nationwide on the effects of environment on various forms of life in all parts—and that includes plants too. For instance, certain plants and flowers, and vegetables too for that matter, will grow in one part of the British Isles and not another. There may be very obvious reasons—like richness of soil or other factors like that, quite simple. But sometimes the reasons are more obscure.'

'How fascinating,' Emma murmured. She wasn't sure if she understood. It sounded very technical.

119

'Like why there are no trees here,' suggested Judith brightly.

Douglas laughed. 'Right. They'd never get a chance in these high winds.' He half turned his head to Philip. 'That's a thought. We could arrange plantings in very sheltered spots and see what happened.'

'Better tell Malcolm. That's his pigeon.'

Emma and Judith exchanged discreet glances. 'That would take years, wouldn't it?' Emma said. 'I mean, you can't stay here for ever, can you?'

'No. Only for a year or so. There'll be others, though. There always are.'

It was all very logical and sensible, but an inner instinct gave Emma a slight feeling of unease. Something wasn't quite right. She had no idea what it was. And both Douglas and Philip were so very pleasant, as indeed the other men seemed. And so welcoming, genuinely so, she would have sworn. She decided her imagination was working overtime again and resolutely tried to put her own inner feelings to one side as she determined to enjoy the rest of the day with its unexpected bonus of a ride out and a visit.

They stopped the Land-Rover at a low spot by a beach, and Douglas turned to both girls. 'Fancy a walk?' he asked them. 'Along this beach are some caves, very eerie and cold. Fine if you're writing a thriller.'

Emma smiled. 'And if you're not?'

'Still fine for a walk. You'll see some seals, and plenty of birds——'

'Oh, don't we need a stick?' Judith asked anxiously, and Philip laughed.

'We'll take care of you. Come on. We'll walk upwards after. I've got some flowers I want you to see.'

They set off, and it was the perfect day for a walk along a beach, and the talk was casual, friendly and natural, as if

120

they had all known each other for ages. Philip, who had seemed rather quiet at first, turned out to be the possessor of a dry wit, and soon Emma had forgotten any faint ideas that had troubled her. She caught Douglas's glance on her several times, and was aware of his interest. She was used to it, but now it was balm to her ego, which Greg Halcro had so effectively bruised. His final remark only hours before, that she couldn't even kiss properly, had wounded her more than she cared to admit even to herself, and Douglas's mild admiration was proving an effective antidote.

They wandered in the caves while Judith, professing her reluctance, stayed outside with Philip. The first cave went back a long way, and there was a current of fresh cold air blowing down on them as they turned a bend. It was dark, yet a faint speck of bright light showed somewhere overhead and she turned to her companion. 'I can see what you mean,' she said. 'I think I've seen enough. There's a *light*.'

Douglas laughed. 'There's a very narrow way up,' he told her. 'Care to try it?'

Emma shivered. 'No, thanks—I'd get claustrophobia. Can we go out now?'

'Of course. Come on. This way.' He took her hand, which seemed very natural, for it was difficult to see anything, although they could hear the sea very faintly, and the others' voices from the beach. He released her hand just before they reached the mouth of the cave, and there had been nothing to it, he had only been guiding her after all, but Emma sensed that if they had stayed any longer in that black eerie place, he would have tried to kiss her. She didn't want that, but she didn't know why. She wanted no entanglements, however innocuous.

After leaving the beach they climbed a sharp path upwards, and here were tall ancient rocks, and a profusion of wild flowers growing at the base, all colours, pinks pre-

121

dominating, and Philip bent and pointed out the different ones, careful as he touched them, telling them names that were familiar and unfamiliar, pointing out as they walked along in the hot sun—moss campion, wild thyme, clover and thrift. And mixed in among them, adding splashes of yellow, blue and white, celandine, violets, daisies and cow parsley. His enthusiasm came across to Emma, who knelt beside him at a marshy spot on their walk as he gently pointed to more varieties. He named them all, and she, who had little knowledge of wild flowers, was immediately confused. Which had been the stitchwort, which the bog bean? They saw many birds, but Douglas named them all—the *swabbie*, Shetland name for a great black-backed gull, soaring effortlessly overhead, keeping a watchful eye on them, gannets, Arctic tern, the island abounded with many different varieties.

And yet they saw no other human beings. There were crofts—but all empty, some in good condition, others in ruins. Emma turned to Douglas as they made their way back towards the Land-Rover after what had been a long leisurely walk.

'Are there many people living here?' she asked. He and Philip exchanged glances.

'Only us.'

She shivered. 'How odd! There are very few people on Skeila either, and all old.'

'This is a remote part of Shetland, don't forget. The young ones move away, the old people die.' He shrugged. 'That's life.'

'But how sad,' said Emma. They could see the vehicle waiting for them, shimmering slightly with the heat, and she suddenly felt very tired. It was nearly five, and she decided it was hunger. And they had both been going to have a rest after their picnic lunch! How far away that seemed now.

Philip drove back to their small encampment, and Emma was very conscious of Douglas sitting behind her, and once a faint whisper touched the back of her neck, and she put up her hand to brush it away, for it must have been a hair, and heard his soft amused chuckle.

The men were waiting. Tom opened the passenger door. 'We've tea ready,' he said. 'A high tea in honour of our lady guests.' He helped them both out. 'If you'll come this way.' The bare shed he took them into was one they had seen from the outside, and it was like an army hut inside with a long trestle table and folding wooden chairs. But someone had set the table, and taken trouble with it, for a vase of mixed flowers stood in the centre. A strange vase. Emma looked more closely, and it was a milk bottle that had been covered with white paper and sellotape.

'Well, we're not used to company,' Malcolm explained as she hid the smile. 'I'll show you the washroom. Just the next hut. There's plenty of hot water if you want to wash.'

He left them and went back, and inside the small washroom with its shower and bath, Judith turned to Emma, eyes alight with laughter. 'What a funny place,' she said. 'Wait till I tell John all about our day's picnic!'

Emma put down her bag and ran water into the spartan-looking washbowl. 'As long as he doesn't get the wrong ideas,' she said, and splashed her face and hands. 'Ah, that's better.' Someone had put a clean towel out for them. It was a khaki colour.

'I doubt it. He'll be interested, more than anything. I'll have him wanting to come up here for a holiday himself soon.'

Emma was drying herself. 'You'll be very welcome anytime,' she said. 'I'll give you the key whenever you want it.' And she added: 'I can just see Greg trying to bully John!'

'What a thought,' Judith smiled. 'You know, oddly enough, I think they'd probably get on well.' She began to wash herself. That was food for thought for Emma. Robert had never particularly liked John, and she sensed the feeling was mutual. And she realized with a jolt that that was the first time she had thought of Robert for a day or so.

They walked back to the dining hut, and there was ham and tongue, and salad on their plates, and five men waiting. The meal was tasty, and everyone talked, and afterwards, the table was cleared away before the girls had a chance to offer. There was a plain bar in the corner, and a record player, and bottles appeared as if by magic from behind that counter, and they were asked what they would like to drink, and it was all so very pleasant that Emma thought it must be all a dream. But it wasn't.

Someone put the record player on after a while, and Douglas asked Emma to dance, which she laughingly did, and it was like a small bar somewhere, with a pleasant atmosphere. And she forgot completely about Greg Halcro, her neighbour. But not for long. For a strange thing happened later on that was to remind her sharply and in a curious way of him.

They had not intended to stay long, but Judith became engrossed in a conversation with Malcolm and Tom because they knew the firm that John worked for and were asking about him, and that was a subject of which Judith never tired, as Emma knew. She had had several dry sherrys and was pleasantly warm and happy, and her watch had stopped, but it didn't seem to matter.

Douglas had showed them round the sheds, after they had eaten, all except one shed which he told them was always kept locked, but as it contained only dull equipment and tools, they weren't missing anything. She looked round from her conversation with Philip and Tom. They seemed

124

fascinated with her modelling experiences, as Tom had assured her his fiancée had always yearned to be a model, and seemed to think it was an easy life. Emma was disillusioning him on that score. Douglas had vanished, and she wondered where he had gone, and hoped it wasn't the washroom, because that was where she intended going.

She stood up. 'Will you excuse me?' she asked them, and sailed out, only very slightly unsteadily. The washroom was empty. She made sure by knocking loudly. Then on her way out, she paused. The locked shed was right behind her, and she was curious, because if it held only dull equipment, why was it the one with that huge television-type aerial? A little peep through the windows wouldn't hurt anyone, and she was concealed from the dining hall by another shed at an angle.

She walked over slowly—and then realized why she could see nothing anyway, for the windows were blacked out. She was just about to turn away when she heard Douglas's voice from inside the shed—and saw that the door was slightly ajar. She paused, knowing she should just go back, because eavesdropping was despicable. But his words held her. He was speaking perfectly naturally, as if confident he couldn't be overheard. 'We're sure they're all right—or nearly.' There was a pause, a short silence, then he said again: 'You think you'll find anything?' Was he on the phone? It seemed so. Again the pause, as he listened, then: 'Okay, will do. A day should be enough, shouldn't it? You're a dark horse, not telling us what they were like. The blonde's a belter——' And Emma knew, she just *knew*, that she and Judith were the ones being talked about. And she couldn't have moved away if she had wanted to now. More silence, then: 'And you'll do it properly?' Emma's heart beat fast. This was like a bad dream. Then she heard the words again. 'I'm sure you're not, but we don't want to arouse their doubts—if there is anything. All right, we'll leave it to you, and I'll fix it this end. I'll be in touch.' He was finishing the call. Quick as a shadow Emma moved away, frightened lest she make a noise, and ran back to the bar where everything was nice and pleasant, and not at all puzzling. Her head ached, but when Douglas came in a few minutes later, she was back to normal. She even managed to smile at him when he asked her to dance, and got up slowly.

'We really must be going back,' she said. 'Really. It's been very nice, but it must be getting late, and it's a long walk from the old ruin to my house——'

'No problem,' he said. 'You don't think we'd let you walk all that way, do you?' and he grinned down at her so boyishly and charmingly that she wondered if she'd imagined what she had overheard. 'I'll run you both round in the boat to your house.'

She hadn't thought of that. 'That's a relief,' she admitted. 'I never thought we'd make it otherwise.'

'No. You've been danced off your feet, haven't you? You don't mind, do you? It's a treat for us poor working lads to get the chance.'

Emma laughed. 'I've enjoyed it. Truly. And so has Judith.' She wished she could ask him about the conversation she had overheard. He was so nice, so genuinely friendly, not in a wolfish way, but just *right*. She was sure he could make it all right—but something held her back, and she didn't know what it was.

They danced and talked for a while longer, then Tom made coffee because both Judith and Emma were beginning to yawn, and it was really time to go. But Judith didn't know about the phone call, or whatever it had been. She thought they were all very nice, you could tell. The coffee was good and hot, from somewhere Philip had found a guitar and strummed it softly while they drank. And it seemed almost sad that they had to leave.

The boat puttered into silence. The *Maria* was at her mooring, and Douglas drew up alongside, and jumped out to pull the smaller boat near the beach. He helped both girls out. 'Have you remembered everything?' he asked, handing them their macs. 'Shall I come up to the house with you?'

'We're fine, thanks.' Emma smiled at him. That phone call, whatever it had been, didn't seem half so important now, there was a perfectly logical explanation for it, she felt sure, and anyway, too many sherrys left the image of the day slightly blurred at the edges, so that it was a golden hazy memory.

'Good. Er——' he seemed slightly hesitant, 'I have to go into Lerwick tomorrow for some supplies. Would you both care for a day out?'

They looked at one another. What a marvellous opportunity for some weekend shopping. 'Yes, please,' Emma answered promptly for them both.

'Fine. About nine? We'll not be back late. Well, I'll best be away back to the others, or they'll think I'm lost. Goodnight.'

They watched him go, and set off walking upwards. Judith said: 'Isn't that lovely? A day out.'

A day out. The words triggered off something in Emma's mind. A day out. That was what Douglas had said on the phone. She looked at Judith. But there was nothing she could say about it. She would think Emma was imagining things again. Perhaps she was. She resolutely put it out of her mind. But one tiny niggling question remained. Who had Douglas been talking to?

# CHAPTER EIGHT

THE day came in with a grey mist that seemed as if it would never go away. Emma wondered if Douglas might not come, but both girls prepared themselves anyway, and Emma slipped out at eight to put the blankets in Greg's porch. She didn't want to see him. A dog stirred inside, and barked, and she scurried back quickly lest he came to his door. How ridiculous, she told herself. She would have to face him some time. But she didn't want it to be just yet. Nothing must spoil their day out, and the sight of him, with the memories, might do that.

They ate breakfast, made the beds and tidied so that by a quarter to nine they were ready and waiting for their visitor. The mist swirled round the house, but it wasn't particularly cold, nor damp, and was already thinning as they looked out of the window. 'He'll come,' Judith said with confidence.

Emma looked at her and smiled. 'He better had,' she answered. 'With that list you've prepared, you'll never get all that stuff from Mr. Grant's. I only hope we don't over-load the boat.' She added doubtfully: 'That's a thought! It was bad enough in Dougall's—oh lor', I hope we're not seasick!'

But they had a pleasant surprise a few minutes later. There came a knock at the door, and Emma went to open it.

'Morning, madame.' Douglas stood there, tall, handsome and smiling. 'There are so many houses hereabouts I'm working my way along them. You never told me where you lived.' He nodded in the direction of the first, ruined one. 'Your neighbours must be away. They didn't answer.'

'You're not one of these door-to-door salesmen, are you?' Emma asked anxiously. How absurd ever to have worried about him!

'Well, I do have a little line in boats. Care to see it?'

'Come in.' She stood back. 'I'm a sucker for boats. Want a coffee before we leave?'

'Just had one. Don't let me stop you, though.'

'No. We're ready. Judith has a shopping list.' She pulled a face. 'I hope the boat won't sink.'

'I heard that.' Judith came in from the kitchen. 'Take no notice of her, Douglas. If anyone comes back loaded with things, it'll be Emma.'

He held up his hands. 'Please! No quarrelling. You can both shop to your hearts' content. You didn't think I'd take you in that little rowing boat, did you?' The quick glance between the two girls answered his question for him, and he laughed. 'You're in for a shock. Your friend's boat, *Maria*, has got nothing on mine, I assure you.'

Five minutes later they saw it, moored alongside Greg Halcro's, and it was a surprise—equally sleek, of similar size, but with the name *Vanessa II* on the side.

'I wonder who Vanessa One was,' murmured Emma to Judith as they scrambled down to the beach. Douglas helped them aboard.

'Make yourselves at home. Lerwick, here we come,' he said, and opened the throttle. With a roar they were off. Judith went to sit down. Emma remained beside Douglas at the controls, fascinated.

'Want a go?' he asked her, after a few minutes in which Skeila grew rapidly smaller, and the mist became wispy, and dispersed.

'May I? It's not your boat, is it?' she asked. She took the

129

wheel, and for a moment Douglas's hands were on hers as he assisted her to get a firm grip.

He laughed. 'Do I look wealthy? No, it's Tom and Malcolm's. We share it while we're up here.'

The wind blew her hair round her face and into her eyes and he reached across and pulled it out of the way. 'I've got a scarf in my bag,' she said. 'I'd better get it.'

'Stay there. I will.' He had gone, and she experienced a moment of panic at being left in sole charge. Yet there was an exhilaration too, and she suddenly sensed the fascination that a boat could hold. Something she had not realized before. Boats were like planes; for getting places. There was beauty and power here, and when he returned with her scarf, she said:

'This is marvellous!'

'Isn't it? You didn't know what you'd been missing, did you?'

She looked at him. A simple sentence, the words lightly meant, deserving a casual answer, which she gave as she laughingly agreed. But there was a deeper truth there, for she hadn't known what she had been missing in life until she came to this place. Despite everything, in spite of the aggressive man who lived next door, and the fact that she seemed quite unable to escape or forget him, even for a short time, she had never known such contentment as she had found on Skeila. Life in London would never be quite the same again. Life in London ... What a strange thought to have.

'Penny for them?'

'What? Oh, sorry, Douglas, I was miles away.'

'I know. And when you're steering one of these things you're supposed to treat it with a little respect.'

'Yes, sir, sorry, sir.' She grinned at him. He was nice. She had forgotten about the phone call. Nearly.

'And don't be cheeky!'

'I'm not.' She tried to look hurt. 'You are the skipper, after all.'

'Hmm. Just as long as you remember,' he said sternly. 'Or I'll send you below to make coffee.'

'You want some?'

'If you do. Can you manage on your own?'

'Of course. Right away—sir,' and she relinquished the wheel and turned away, smiling.

Whether his boat was faster than Dougall's was not certain, but the journey certainly seemed to be accomplished in less time. Perhaps it was the company. It didn't matter. Emma saw Lerwick grow larger as they approached a small harbour, saw the tall buildings, a square church spire with a clock on it slightly further away, people talking by the boats, a blue and white bus waiting for passengers, and gulls everywhere.

Douglas wove in between the many boats that were moored there, and the sun shone high and bright in a clear sky, and the waters of the harbour were still and calm, and everything was perfect.

'Look, I thought I'd leave you to do your shopping while I go and arrange our supplies. Say we meet back here in an hour?' Douglas suggested. 'Then we'll pile our stuff on board, and I'll show you a few sights.'

'That sounds fine,' both girls agreed. Emma added: 'What about lunch?'

'We'll have that before we do our grand tour. An hour's shopping should give you an appetite. I know a good hotel near here. Okay?'

They were walking away from the harbour, and at the first street corner Douglas left them. The two girls sauntered along fascinated by the many small shops full of local knitwear, and jewellery and crafts. The road was narrow

131

and twisting, the main shopping area stone-flagged and traffic-free, a pleasant change for them both, and even on the parts with cars, these were infrequent. Judith said: 'It's a bit different from the big city, isn't it?'

'A bit,' Emma agreed dryly. No one seemed to be in any hurry. Women gossiped in shop doorways as they do the world over, but you didn't have to push a way through, there were smiles and nods when the girls wanted to pass. The people were friendly. Maybe, thought Emma, they were used to tourists, and welcomed them. It was fascinating to hear them speak too, with a musical lilt almost to their voices, the way they said 'dis' for 'this'. She could have listened for hours.

They spent some time in a bookshop and each bought a few paperbacks, leaving at last reluctantly, for they both enjoyed reading. Then, loaded with food, postcards and stamps, they made their way back to the harbour. The hour was not quite up. Douglas was standing talking to a man, his back to them. The man was shorter, well built, dressed in sports coat and flannels, wearing a flat cap. As they approached, the man raised his hand in a farewell salute and walked quickly away. Douglas turned to greet them.

'There you are.' He looked at his watch. 'What good timekeepers you are! Five minutes to go. Right, I've got my things on board, let's have yours.' And he took their shopping bags from them and jumped down on deck. When he had vanished into the cabin, Emma said:

'I wonder who that was?'

Judith gave her an amused look. 'I don't know. Why not ask him?'

'It doesn't matter,' Emma said lightly.

They ate lunch in an hotel overlooking the harbour. A gull stood on the window-ledge and watched them eat. Judith passed out a morsel of bread which it pecked greed-

132

ily—and waited for more, beady yellow eyes unwinkingly on them.

'We'll have it following us all day if you keep doing that,' Douglas remarked.

'Good. We'll have it as a pet on Skeila, then,' answered Judith, unabashed.

'Ah, but when you go back to London, what then?'

'Greg can take over,' Emma replied lightly. 'He is the local birdman, after all,' and she smiled at Douglas.

'Perhaps. How long are you here for anyway?'

Emma's toe touched Judith's. 'I don't know. We haven't decided yet, have we?' she looked at her friend. 'You're not trying to get rid of us, like *him*, are you?'

'Me?' he laughed. The softly spoken waitress came up to take away their dinner plates, and he waited until she had gone again. 'Is he trying to get rid of you?'

Emma was sorry that she had said it. She didn't want the day to be spoilt, and Greg Halcro might just manage that, even from a distance of miles. She shook her head, half laughing. 'Just a joke,' she said. 'He doesn't like strangers.'

'Ah. I shouldn't worry. Some men are like that—think they own the place. Don't let him bother you. If I was your next-door neighbour I'd be different, I can tell you.' And the conversation took a different turn. Yet Emma was left with the slightly odd feeling of words left unsaid, of something again that was not quite right.

All was forgotten afterwards as they left the hotel after lunch, and Douglas pointed to a car waiting outside, a bright red Corsair. 'There she is,' he said. 'Come on, get in.' Seeing their astonished faces, he laughed. 'I'm not pinching it,' he assured them. 'The man I was talking to has lent it me for the afternoon. I'm going to take you around the island. This is the best way. We go at our own

133

speed, and I can point out the various places of interest as we go.'

They set off southwards from Lerwick. The names of the streets were fascinating, the Norwegian influence that pervaded the place echoed in them: Olaf Street, King Harald Street, St. Magnus Street. And as they travelled the narrow well surfaced roads, Douglas gave them a potted history of the Shetlands, not in a schoolmasterly manner, but casually, making it seem really fascinating. 'There's an uninhabited island not far away called Noss,' he said. 'It has a bird sanctuary there, and some terrific cliffs. I bet your friend Greg Halcro has been there.'

'I'll ask him when we get back,' said Emma dryly. She was sitting beside Douglas, and Judith sat happily in the back of the car, which was very comfortable. They went round the spectacularly beautiful island, saw Scalloway Castle, many crofts, some empty, some inhabited, and occasionally a thatched one with wire netting over the thatch to protect it from being lifted away in the gales. The day was warm and dry, the sun high in the sky. They walked along the cliffs at one point and were attacked by a large angry bird which dived down at them in a menacing way. At least, reflected Emma, Greg Halcro had spoken the truth in one respect. Douglas found a stick and they ran laughing back to the car while he skilfully fended it off.

He flung the stick in the back, on the floor. 'We might need that again,' he grinned. 'I told you I'd look after you both.'

'My hero,' Emma murmured, clasping her bosom and fluttering her eyelashes. He looked at her as he started the car.

'That's twice you've been cheeky today,' he said menacingly. 'Just wait!'

'Promises, promises,' she whispered, and he burst out

laughing.

The rest of the trip was accomplished with laughter and jokes as they set off back to Lerwick. He parked by the small boat harbour. 'Now, are there any last-minute purchases you've remembered?' he asked, as he looked at his watch. 'Most of the shops shut at five, so you've got half an hour.'

'Cakes,' Emma said firmly. 'Let's treat ourselves. I saw some gorgeous-looking ones in a shop not far away. Can I go?' She looked at Douglas.

'Of course. Want me to come with you?'

'No, I'll find it. Won't be a minute.' She slammed the door and ran towards the shops. She chose six of the most luscious cream-filled confections she could find, and made her way carefully back, the cakes in their box held in front of her. Two each. I must be mad, she thought, but I don't care, there's time to diet when I go back to London——

'Oh!' The man had turned the corner very suddenly, and a collision, in which the precious cakes would have been squashed, was only averted by him holding out both hands and grasping her arms. She looked up, startled, into a pair of deep brown eyes, a shock of black hair above a tanned face, and the man laughed and said:

'Forgive me.' He was dressed like a seaman, and his accent was neither Scottish nor English, but deep and guttural.

She moved on after smiling, assuring him that no damage had been done, and saw the car—and Douglas watching her from it.

'So what was that about?' he asked lightly.

'I nearly had a nasty accident and lost the cakes,' she said. 'He was foreign. I wonder where from?'

'Russia?' he suggested.

Emma looked sharply at him. 'A Russian?' she exclaimed. 'Oh!'

'Don't look so startled. There are dozens of them here. As well as Norwegians, Danes, French, Poles—take your pick.' And he was looking at her in a very amused way.

She shook her head. 'I don't know. When someone only says "forgive me," ' she made a fair imitation of the accent —'you don't really have time to tell.'

He laughed. 'You should be a mimic. Come on, let's go.'

'Are you just leaving the car here?' Judith asked as she got out.

'Sure. He'll come and collect it. No one will touch it, if that's what you're worried about.'

They walked along to the boat and he helped them on board. Emma put the cakes securely on a seat before going to join Douglas at the wheel.

'Shall I make us a drink?' she offered.

'If you like. Thanks.'

'It's been a lovely day,' she said. 'Thank you for bringing us.'

'It's been a pleasure, I assure you.'

'You'll stay for a meal when we get back?' and she added: 'I got *two* cakes for you!'

He grinned. 'Do I look half starved? Of course, I'd like to. Thanks.' She went down below and put on the kettle. There was something very satisfying, she reflected, about life on board a boat. Very peaceful and calm—in the right weather. She wondered how long it would take them to get back.


Douglas stayed until nearly ten talking to them before saying he would really have to go, or the others would be sending out search parties for him. As they walked towards the beach, he asked Emma: 'Would you both like another trip out on Sunday? Just a short one in the afternoon?'

'We'd love to, thanks.' Emma saw Judith's slight smile, and guessed what was going through her friend's mind. They waved him off and set off back to the cottage.

'Look, Judith, it's not like you think,' Emma hastened to reassure her friend.

'No?' Judith began to laugh. 'How do you know what I'm thinking?'

'I know *you*. I like him, but only as a friend, that's all.'

'Of course,' Judith answered soothingly. 'Well, I might just have a headache on Sunday. I could do with a day off after all this excitement—out to tea and dancing yesterday, a boat trip today—London won't half seem tame after all this lot!'

'Now *there's* a thought! Come to the Shetlands for excitement and adventure!'

'And you'll never be the same again.'

'No. Never the same——' Emma stopped. Funny that Judith should say that. She felt different, had done since she came, and there had been a subtle change with each day that passed. She went up to her bedroom to bring down some clothes she had left in a corner, for washing, while Judith went out to put the kettle on for their bedtime drink. She sat down on the bed to think for a moment. What was it, this difference? She did not know. She was facing her dressing table as she sat, in the place she occupied every day when she made up—or at least applied lipstick, which was all she had bothered about lately. And it was odd, because the mirror was at a different angle from what it had been that morning.

Emma straightened it. That was better. That was how it should be. But how strange. Why should a heavy mirror move when there was no one there to move it? She stood up and walked across to it. The faint film of dust she hadn't had time to remove that morning was still there. But there was a patch where a jar of face cream had been shifted to one side, a moonshape of dust-free surface. A tingle of something akin to fear touched Emma's spine and prickled the back of her neck.

She slowly opened the top drawer. Everything was in neat order as it had been before. The second drawer was the same. In the bottom one was her small writing case. She lifted it out. The zip always stuck, and it had caught on a scrap of paper the last time she had closed it, after writing to Robert. Holding the case carefully, she looked round it. The scrap of paper was no longer there. Emma sat down on the bed again, still clutching the case, and now her heart beat faster.

Judith could have moved the cream, could have borrowed it—but she wouldn't have gone in Emma's writing case, not without asking first, and she had her own paper anyway. Emma swallowed hard. She quickly opened the tiny top drawer where she kept her rings and various items of jewellery. Everything was there—and yet there was a subtle difference. She didn't know what it was, only that she was becoming more certain with every moment that passed that someone had been through every drawer very carefully. A burglar? On Skeila? It wasn't credible.

She went to the wardrobe and riffled through coats and dresses. They shifted gently as her questing hands moved along, and then settled into place. Nothing was missing. Yet now the feeling grew; someone had searched her room very carefully, but had not taken anything. Who? And the memory of Douglas's phone call came back to her as she stood very still in her room on that warm Friday evening. And he had said something about a day. Was that why he had invited them out to Lerwick for an entire day—to give someone the chance to go through their house and possessions with a fine tooth comb? And there was just one person whose name sprang instantly to mind: Greg Halcro.

Emma went down the stairs. An anger was growing inside her, and she was frightened lest Judith see it, for she didn't want her in any way upset—but she would not sleep until the question had been answered one way or the other. She paused in the living room. Sounds came from the kitchen. Judith was preparing supper. 'I'll not be a minute,' Emma called. 'I'm going to Greg Halcro's.'

'What?' The voice expressed surprise. 'What for?'

Only a second to think. 'To tell him about the bird sanctuary on Noss, and ask him if he wants that book back yet.'

'Well, don't be long.'

'I won't.' No, I won't, she added grimly to herself. It shouldn't take long to ask him—although she wasn't sure what she would do when he answered.

The anger grew. It was a white-hot spark inside her, and there was the horrible feeling of having been used—Douglas too—he was in it. Hard to believe, for he had never been anything but nice to them both—and yet everything seemed to be falling into a pattern, and it was not a pleasant one.

She knocked at his door. The light shone out, and there was music from inside. Then he was at the door, and he looked faintly surprised.

'Good evening,' he said. 'I got the blankets safely.'

'I didn't come about those. Are you going to ask me in?'

'If you wish,' he stood aside and Emma walked in. The two dogs lay on the rug in front of the fire. The stereo played soft music in the corner, and a cup of tea stood by the chair which held a book. A domestic scene, and one which made her feel an intruder. But things had gone too far now. There would be no leaving, the anger was solid and real, and she was only frightened that she would lose her temper. She took a deep breath. No use asking—did you search my room? because he would say no. She had to pretend she knew.

'You left something behind when you searched the house today,' she said, and she kept her eyes firmly on his face for the slightest flicker of reaction. Which there was—but it was no guilt, merely surprise as he raised a questioning eyebrow and said:

'When I did *what*?'

'You heard me. You broke into Craig House today, and looked through everything.'

'You must be mad.' He said it flatly, calmly.

She wanted to shake him. 'I'm not,' she said. 'You are. Do I look stupid? I heard Douglas phoning you yesterday —and then he invited us out to Lerwick, and we went, and while we were there you broke in——'

'Just a moment,' he interrupted. 'How did I break in— and who the hell is Douglas?'

'It shouldn't be any trouble to you—and don't pretend you don't know him, because he knows you, he's tall and fair and good-looking——'

'Spare me the details,' he said. 'But just one little thing, dear girl. I have not got a telephone.' He said those last six words very slowly and clearly.

For a moment Emma was floored. Then she found her voice. Because it had gone too far now—she could not back down. 'No,' she said. 'I don't care. It could have been a radio receiver, then.' And her eyes went to the stairs, which lay behind the living room. If only she could look . . .

'This gets more melodramatic every minute,' he remarked, and sounded almost amused, almost bored. And if he was telling the truth, she reasoned, he'd be hopping mad at her accusations, not tolerant like this, for whatever else

140

he was, he wasn't a tolerant person. She mentally measured the distance to the stairs. If she could make it . . .

'Oh,' she moaned. 'I feel faint,' and she put her hand to her forehead and swayed slightly. 'M-may I have a glass of w-water?' She saw his hesitation, the long cool look he gave her, and sat down quickly on a chair.

With a muttered oath he turned and went out into the kitchen. Quick as a flash, Emma was up the stairs.

Swiftly to the back bedroom—everything in his house was the same way round as hers, so that was easy—the door—the door was locked—and Greg Halcro was pounding up after her, now reaching out, swinging her round to face him.

'You crafty little——' he bit back the last word, and Emma looked up at him, saw the dark anger in his eyes, and thoroughly frightened, began to struggle.

'Let me go—let me *go*!'

'Like hell I will! You come here accusing me—pretending to be ill—my God, you're a cool customer——'

'I know you're up to no good—you and all of them—I hate you!' she breathed.

'Listen to me. You must forget all this nonsense——'

'How can I?' Her breathing was ragged and uneven, his hands were tight upon her shoulders, the landing was dark and shadowy, and Emma was afraid. She was more afraid than she had ever been in her life before, with a sweeping wave of crushing helplessness that seemed as if it might overwhelm her. She had to get away from him, and soon, for what might he not do? Yet one thought was uppermost in her mind: Judith. Judith her friend, who could so easily be hurt—'I don't care what you do to me,' she said, 'but please let Judith go. She knows nothing—she thinks I've come to tell you something about a bird sanctuary—but you mustn't hurt her—she's h-having a baby——' the landing

141

was swaying gently, and tingling white sparks filled the shadows, and her head was spinning. She only vaguely heard him begin:

'What sort of monster do you think——' but she didn't hear the rest because the white sparks became a rushing waterfall that filled her head, and she wondered why she was drowning when there was no water, no water at all . . .

'All right, you can stop fighting.' The words came at her from far away, and Emma opened her eyes. She was lying on a bed, and Greg Halcro was watching her from a chair by the bedside. 'You're quite safe,' he said drily. 'I mean, not about to be ravished, or anything approaching it, so just relax.' And he smiled. He actually *smiled*. Her eyes widened. What now? He was better when he was angry. She knew where she was then.

'Do you want to sit up?'

'Yes.' But she did it by herself before he could help her.

'Right,' he said. 'I thought your faint was another bit of the acting lark—until you went an absolute dead weight on me—then I knew it wasn't.' He stopped. 'I think,' he went on slowly, 'the time has come for us to have a little talk.'

But suddenly Emma didn't want to know any more. 'No,' she began. 'No, I want to go——'

'Not yet. Not yet, love.'

She looked round her at the spartanly furnished room. He had called her love. Now wasn't that a funny thing when he hated her?

'You're right. I did go through your house, and all your possessions today—and your friend Judith's too. And Douglas was in on it—and it was me he was speaking to yesterday—not on the phone, but as you so aptly guessed, on a radio receiver—and I have been trying to get rid of you, but I'm not any more.'

It was one thing to imagine things, to picture them in your mind—it was quite another to hear them confirmed in cool calm measured words. Emma dared not speak. She took a deep breath. Greg gave her a half smile, sensing her feelings. 'No questions?' he asked gently.

'You're going to tell me why?'

'Yes, I am. That much I owe you. I'm sorry I had to do it—it's not to my taste, believe me. But it was necessary.'

'Why?' It was an anguished plea. Why did her heart ache so?

'Because we didn't know who you were—we weren't sure of you. And everything you did seemed to lead me—us—to think that you were up to no good——'

'I don't understand,' she burst out. 'I can't believe——' she felt almost ill.

'I think we'd better go downstairs. That cup of tea will be cold. I'll make more—and one for you. Come on.'

Emma swung her feet over the side of the bed and stood up. 'Can you manage?' he asked.

'Yes, thank you.'

He went down, followed by Emma. She went into the kitchen after him, no longer sure of herself. He pulled out a kitchen chair from under the table. 'Sit down. It won't be a minute, and then we can talk,' he said.

'What about Judith?' Emma asked. 'I said I wouldn't be away long.'

'She might as well hear. Shall we go to your house?'

'I don't—I don't know. She's not——' she stopped.

Greg grinned. 'I'm not going to shock either of you,' he said. 'Not enough to scare you—or her. We'd better go.' He switched off the gas. 'Come on.'

Judith was surprised to see them both. Her eyes widened as Greg followed Emma in, but unflappable as ever, she

143

merely said: 'I'll make another cup of coffee. Won't be a moment.'

He waited until she returned. 'I owe you both an explanation,' he began. 'Just stop me if you get to a part that doesn't make sense. Okay?'

They nodded. 'Right,' he said. 'Then I'll begin. You've been suspicious about me from the start, Emma, and rightly so. I'm not writing a book on birds, and Douglas and his little crowd are no more naturalists than you're Chinese. We are all here working for the Government, and quite frankly, it was thought that you two might just have been beautiful spies!'

# CHAPTER NINE

AFTER that first startling announcement, he had an attentive audience for everything that followed. Emma and Judith had looked wordlessly at each other, and then, still in silence, groped for their beakers of coffee.

Greg smiled. 'All right,' he said. 'Maybe I put it a bit strong, but believe me, you've both caused a great deal of anguish and heart-searching in this neck of the woods. Quite innocently, of course—as we now know—but we didn't at first. And we had to be sure of you.' He looked at Judith. 'And you helped there, more than a little. That letter from your husband, John——'

'Yes?' She sat up straight, and Greg winced.

'I'm sorry, Judith. Truly sorry. But I had the address, and him, checked today, and he's on Government work too, isn't he?'

'Yes, but I don't see the connection——' Judith began.

'No. But you will in a minute. He's been thoroughly vetted, as you have too—and your close friends. We know that.' He looked at Emma. 'Which puts you in the clear too—although we double checked you, and you're exactly who you say you are—a top London model, hard-working and successful, and niece of the man who used to live here——'

'Just a minute,' Emma interrupted. 'You're telling us a lot of things about us. What about *you*? What sort of Government work are you involved in that makes you so worried about spies? Spies!' she repeated scornfully. 'I've never heard anything so ridiculous——'

145

'Wait. Please,' he said. He had a very nice smile when he tried. 'You've heard of the Early Warning System, haven't you? Stretching up from Turkey through Europe, and up to here—in the Shetlands. It constitutes a virtually unbroken curtain to protect America and the Western Nato powers from sudden missile attack from the East.' He stopped to sip his coffee and take out his cigarettes. There was no interruption from Emma this time. The deadly seriousness of his tone was enough. 'There are also monitoring establishments as well here. Their job is simply to eavesdrop on all radio communication among Russian trawlers and anyone who's prowling about on the high seas.' He lit a cigarette after first offering the packet to the girls. 'We're all part of the link—me only in a minor way, Douglas and Tom and the others slightly more directly. I can't tell you much more, for obvious reasons, but I assure you that your arrival was an event I hadn't foreseen. I'm used to being on my own here, getting on with things my own way. You made a shrewd point, Emma, when you said there were only old people here. Quite true. And they leave me alone, because I've built up an image of an eccentric bird-watcher —although I get on with most of the villagers when I'm there. Mrs. Stevenson's son now, you can imagine where he's working—which is why I interrupted you that day. I keep an eye on her for Ian. Visit her once a week or so— and I swear it was just coincidence that day I arrived just after you—but you seemed to be getting around too much for my liking.'

'Why did Douglas invite us over to their camp if their work is so secret?' Judith asked thoughtfully.

He laughed. 'There was nothing for you to see. If you'd been up to no good, what better way to lull your suspicions? Their naturalist cover is very good. Philip, for instance, is an expert on wild flowers——'

146

They both nodded in agreement, remembering their visit to the island, and his obvious knowledge and love of plants. 'And Malcolm, if he was called on, could bore your socks off about land formations and sub-strata. You'd have come away with your heads reeling with facts and figures—and no doubt a few rock samples.'

The first astonishment and disbelief were gradually wearing away. So much was becoming clear now. So very much. Emma looked at Greg, and he even seemed different in appearance now that the wall of prickly hostility had vanished. Her heart stirred. She had accused him of so many things, yet he had been none of these, merely a man with a difficult job to do. And how must he have felt when he found her on board his boat at night? She shuddered.

'Greg,' she said, 'I owe you an apology. When I went on board the *Maria* that night, I thought you were a—criminal of some sort.'

'I know. You made that clear—and at the same time you gave me even more mixed feelings about you, I can promise you that.'

She looked down at her hands, suddenly wishing she hadn't spoken, suddenly remembering the kisses afterwards ...

He went on, rather quickly, as if perhaps guessing her thoughts: 'So that's why, when Douglas was reporting to me about your visit, I suggested the day out. I intended going through this house with a fine tooth comb, and I did. All I found were the letters, then I went home and checked with London——' he shrugged. 'The rest you know.'

Judith stood up. 'I don't know about you,' she said, 'but I'm going to have another cup of coffee. Want one?' She looked at them both.

'Please.' They said it together, then looked at one another, and smiled.

'Can we get one thing straight?' said Emma lightly, because just at that moment she didn't want to get on serious subjects, she didn't know why. 'Douglas has asked us out on the boat on Sunday. That's not another part of the plot, is it?'

Greg raised one eyebrow. 'Not the kind you mean, no,' he assured her. 'Although maybe Douglas——' and he stopped and shook his head faintly. 'Never mind.'

Emma was intrigued. 'Tell me,' she asked.

He shrugged. 'Well, I should imagine it's for entirely personal reasons.' And then he grinned.

'Oh!' Silly question—so why did she feel a little piqued at his casual, disinterested answer?

It was later, as she lay in bed, that she realized why. She had been annoyed at his obvious lack of concern as to whether she went out with Douglas or not because she wanted Greg to be jealous. Jealous! Emma sat up in bed. Her head ached terribly. Not surprising after all that had happened, all the discoveries made that evening. But Greg —jealous? Now why on earth, she thought, should I want that? But the question was already answering itself as she saw his face again, as she remembered their talk—a very serious and surprising talk—downstairs only a short time before. He had been answering a question of Judith's, and Emma had been able to watch him unobserved, and had felt a disturbing pounding in the region of her heart as she looked at that strong face, the dark grey eyes, the animation as he spoke. She had wanted to go on looking at him undisturbed, pleasuring in the sight of him ... The spell had been broken, because he had turned to Emma then, and she had had to quickly compose her features, lest he see. But now, remembering, warmth filled her. She would have liked to reach out and touch him, hold his hand, be kissed ... Don't be stupid, she told herself severely, and punched her

148

pillow into a comfortable softness. Don't be an idiot. Go to sleep. But for some reason, sleep eluded her for quite a long time.

She knew Judith was watching her on Saturday, slightly puzzled, but Emma couldn't talk about the one subject uppermost in her mind. Greg. He was there all the time in her thoughts, refusing to go away. She thought he might come round, but they saw nothing of him all day. Was that, she wondered, why the time passed so slowly, even dragged?

They spoke about their discoveries, of course. Difficult not to, for everything that had puzzled them was made clear now. And Emma explained about the one-sided conversation she had heard, that taken together with the certainty that someone had searched the house had triggered off her suspicions and made her go to Greg as she had. Judith listened, half amused, half astonished when Emma told of her attempt to see Greg's study—the locked room at his house.

'You've got more nerve than me,' she admitted, when Emma had finished. 'Weren't you frightened?'

'Terrified,' agreed Emma. It was late afternoon. They had walked to the village, visited the Grants and the two elderly sisters, and the evening stretched blankly ahead. Emma felt strangely restless, as if she wanted to be alone for a while. She went to the window and looked out. What did she hope to see? Greg passing on his way home? She didn't even know if he was at home or not. She turned away from the window, biting her lip, and Judith said gently:

'Why don't you go for a little walk?'

Emma gave a faint smile. 'Trying to get rid of me?'

'No. But you've been like a cat on hot bricks all day. A walk might do you good—clear your head.' She paused,

149

then added softly: 'It's Greg, isn't it?'

Emma looked at her. 'Does it show?'

Judith laughed. 'Not to anyone else. But I know you very well, remember?'

Emma sat beside her. 'Oh, Judith,' she moaned. 'Aren't I silly? I can't stop thinking about him. What am I to do?'

'Nothing. You'll think of something, love. He'll be round, you see.'

'No.' Emma shook her head. 'He was different last night. I can't explain it, but he was—oh, I don't mean telling us about his job, not just that. You know how hostile he was before? Well, that was gone, you could tell—but somehow he'd changed in a—a different way. There was a kind of blankness—I can't explain it——'

'I think I know what you mean,' Judith said slowly. 'But has it occurred to you—he might think you like Douglas?'

Emma looked at her. She saw again his face, heard his voice as he had said that Douglas was taking them out the following day for 'purely personal reasons'. And she nodded. 'Maybe. But I don't—I mean, I like Douglas, but only as a friend—just someone to talk to, that's all.'

'Hmm, I know,' answered Judith, 'and so do you. But does Greg?'

'I think,' said Emma, with a faint tinge of bitterness, 'I preferred Greg when he was hostile!'

Judith laughed. 'He was more interesting. Go on, go and get your coat and take a brisk walk along the shore. It'll tire you out, and I'll just sit here quietly and write to John.'

'Are you sure?'

'Positive,' was the firm answer. 'Now, scoot.'

Emma set off out. She needed to think, she needed quiet to do so, and out of doors was a stimulating place to do so. She scrambled down to the beach, along the by now familiar path, and set off walking along the shore. A sharp cool wind blew in from the dark water, and everything was quiet. Even the gulls appeared to be asleep, and there was no sign of Greg's boat. Perhaps he was with the other men on Eskla. Working? She shivered. There was something rather mysterious about the fact that they had come on a perfectly ordinary holiday and found themselves thrown in the middle of a place where it appeared that they had been suspected of being up to no good. And she had thought Greg to be a smuggler!

Emma sat on a rock and threw a pebble in the water. A black shape heaved itself from the sea, a distance away, a shiny dark shadow that vanished almost immediately without a ripple—probably a seal or a porpoise. Philip would have known. The sky was a faint yellow with tinges of red washed across it, and on the horizon a boat appeared briefly, then vanished over the skyline, much, she thought, as the seal had done. A quietness descended on Emma, and she sat there scarcely moving, trying to get her thoughts into some kind of order. You cannot, she told herself firmly, carry on mooning over a man who is clearly not interested in you.

But it's easier said than done, came the following thought immediately afterwards. Much easier. Another full week, and then they must leave this beautiful place—and she wouldn't see Greg again. Or at least not until the next visit. But he might have moved on then. A cold sensation seized her at that. How awful to come all this way, with a certain thought, a hope in your heart—only to see his house forlorn and empty. A tear trickled down her cheek. Oh, what a funny life it was! Emma looked up at the sky. She had grown temporarily tired of the feverish rat-race, and come up to escape for a while, hoping to go back refreshed. Instead, how hollow it would all seem on her return. There would be work to do, and parties, nights out, holidays—a busy whirl—but not what she wanted.

Because she had fallen in love with a tall dark Viking of a man who had shown her what a *real* man could be like. He had told her that she didn't even know how to kiss properly. Those words still had the power to hurt even after the aeons of time that seemed to have passed since their utterance. He was cruel too. Cruel and hard—but she sensed that he could also be gentle. Not that I'm likely to see that side of him, she thought wryly. She picked up a flat pebble and flung it idly into the water, where it vanished with a faint plop.

A dreadful loneliness came over her. She stood up. Useless to stay here for ever. Thinking got you nowhere—only made things worse. She set off walking. Douglas would be there tomorrow, and they would have a day out, and on Monday they might go another picnic, perhaps explore the ruined castle they had not really seen round before, because of Douglas's interruption . . .

'Well, well. All alone?' The man's voice startled her. She looked round surprised, and Greg scrambled down to the beach beside her, followed by his two dogs, and for a horrible moment she wondered if her thoughts had been aloud. Her heartbeats quickened, and she pulled her coat round her as if cold, because he made her feel so confused.

'Yes,' she answered. 'Judith's writing a letter. Not out on a fishing trip tonight?'

'Not tonight,' he agreed, straight-faced.

She didn't know what to say—it was absurd—but she suddenly felt like a tongue-tied schoolgirl, and the next words were uttered in sheer self-defence, although she would never know fully why. 'We're leaving here in a few days,' she said.

'Really?' he was beside her now, slowing his footsteps to match hers while the dogs bounded ahead along the sand.

'The bright lights calling?'

'Yes.' She had regained her composure now, Let him see you don't care, she told herself. 'It's very nice here, but too quiet for a city girl like myself.' He had once called her that, she remembered. So she laughed, to let him see that didn't matter either.

He gave her an odd look, and she returned the glance with equanimity. Something was there in the air, a certain tension growing again between them, but she didn't want it. She didn't want him to discover the reason, because he made it obvious he didn't care a bit. 'I should imagine it is,' he said, only the faintest tinge of irony in his words. 'The odd boat trip can't compare with all those night clubs and sparkling restaurants, can it?'

'You put it so nicely,' she said. 'But I wouldn't keep my job for long if I spent every evening dining and dancing, I assure you.'

'No,' he agreed gravely. 'Your looks are an asset, of course. Although some of those models in the posh mags I've seen look as though a few good meals would do them no harm. I can't see any attraction in skinny women.'

She couldn't put her finger on anything precisely, but she sensed that in some way he was taking a certain pleasure in trying to needle her. For reasons of his own no doubt, and she was determined not to let him see that he was succeeding. But it was difficult, very difficult.

'That's your opinion,' she said, 'and you're quite entitled to it—but then I'd hardly call you a typical reader of what you call "posh mags".'

'True.' Was he trying not to laugh? 'Are you?'

'Am I what?'

'A typical reader of them?'

'I enjoy looking at them, of course,' she shrugged. 'Most women do. But I didn't come out for a walk to talk shop.' I came to think about you, she added silently. And wasn't that ironic?

'Do forgive me,' he murmured. 'It's so difficult to know what to talk about—me a simple country boy and all——'

'You're not funny!' she snapped, stung on the raw.

He laughed. 'That's better. I'm not used to having polite conversations—are you?'

'I don't know what you mean,' and she quickened her footsteps imperceptibly.

'Oh yes, you do,' he answered. 'It's been one running battle between us ever since you came—don't let's spoil the record now——'

'And whose fault is that?' she whirled round on him. 'Yours! You—you——' she couldn't find appropriate words. 'You make me laugh. Do you think I care? Personally I prefer you as you were before, all hostile and aggressive—oh yes, you were,' she added, as he put up a protesting hand, as if to interrupt her, 'so don't pretend otherwise. I can remember your face when I first came and saw my house. You were delighted at the state it was in—but at least I knew where I was with you. So let's keep it that way, shall we?'

'Wow!' He gave a long low whistle. 'Atta-girl! That's my Emma——'

'I am *not* your Emma!' she said, teeth clenched. The whole situation was getting completely out of hand. But if he thought——

'Obviously not. It was a figure of speech, for which I must crave your pardon. I didn't realize how offensive it is to you——'

'Yes, it is! Don't be damn patronising! Who do you think you are?' she demanded.

'Oh, I know who I am. Thanks. I don't think you're so sure, though. Look at you, all a-quiver with righteous indignation just because someone makes a joking remark——'

'It wasn't "someone" who made it. It was you—and there's the difference. All your remarks are insulting, if you know what I think, not joking.' Everything was so quiet around them, the dogs had vanished, and there was not another soul about. And the two figures on the beach faced one another, the tall slender girl, the taller broader man, two dark outlines silhouetted against the line of sea and sky, with the long twilight, the "simmer dim" all about them, bathing them in soft cool light. There were so many words to be said, but they could not be. Not then.

'And I do know exactly who I am too, thank you. I'm sure you think you're terribly important up here, and no one else counts. Well, let me tell you, Mr. Greg Halcro, you're mistaken. The world doesn't revolve round you and your job, so there!' she finished childishly.

He began to laugh softly. 'You know,' he remarked, 'it's really tempting when you're mad—I mean the urge to kiss you—if only to shut you up.'

'Don't try it!' Her fists clenched. 'I've not forgotten what you said about *that*. Touch me and I swear I'll hit you!'

'What did I say?' He seemed genuinely interested and puzzled.

'You—you t-told me——' it was difficult to say the words, 'that I didn't even know how to kiss properly.'

'I said that?' he appeared surprised. 'How ungallant!'

'Yes.' And she turned away and began walking. Funny how you could love and hate a person at the same time. But you could, because that was exactly what she felt at that moment, a mixture of both emotions, a desire to hurt him.

'How cruel of me.' He had caught up with her and took her arm to hold her still.

'Yes, it was.' She stood there and looked hard at him. 'Let go of my arm—now!'

155

'You're hopping mad,' he said.

'Not at all. Your opinion of me is so unimportant that it doesn't count——'

'I don't believe you,' he said softly.

'So you're calling me a liar now? Thanks.' She accented the last word.

'Not exactly. But unless you're completely indifferent to someone, you're bound to be interested in what they think about you—and you're not indifferent to me.'

What did he mean? He couldn't have guessed—that was too awful to contemplate. She went on quickly—too quickly: 'No, I'm not. I don't—don't like you.'

'Well, that's truthful anyway.'

'Yes, it is. So will you let me go?'

He took his hand away from her arm. Emma didn't move. She didn't want to, but didn't know why.

'Well, off you go, little girl. You're free now. See?' He held up the hand that had imprisoned her. 'Go and have your walk on your own.'

Without another word, Emma turned and walked quickly away. She didn't look back, because she sensed that he was watching her. Yet when she scrambled up loose stony soil to the cliff top she risked a look around, a quick sideways glance. He had vanished completely, and so had the dogs.

Douglas made a token protest, a polite plea, when Judith insisted that she had a headache on Sunday. But she was adamant, and eventually they left, Emma feeling a mixture of unhappiness and defiance at the prospect of a day out with Douglas, whom she liked—but he wasn't Greg. It was as simple as that. He was not Greg. Strange, because every time they met the sparks flew, the fur, metaphorically speaking, bristled, and yet deep down, in spite of it all, she knew he was one man she could not, would not ever forget.

156

Douglas was good company, interesting, but there was no magic spark of attraction—at least not on Emma's part. She knew that Douglas liked her a great deal.

Damn Greg, she thought. I'm going to enjoy myself today. And she set out to do just that. Douglas had brought food and drink, and they set off in his boat, and Emma smiled to herself as she watched his hands at the wheel. Did he knew of Greg's revelations of the Friday evening? Quite possibly not. She decided to tease him.

She sighed and looked at him. 'Found any interesting plants lately?' she asked very innocently.

'Well, we keep busy, you know,' and he grinned at her.

'Oh, I know you do,' and she gave him a sweet smile. 'Do you have to send reports and things to your—er—employers?'

'Yes. It's all go. I'm being a bit cheeky taking the day off to take you out,' he told her. He looked very attractive in white sweater and dark jeans, and Emma idly went through a mental list of her friends who might care for a week or so on Skeila . . .

'Heavens, I am honoured,' she said. 'What part of England are you from?'

'I'm a Lancashire lad,' he answered. 'Manchester. Why?'

She shrugged. 'Just curious. I was there for a photographic session once. It rained.'

He laughed. 'That rumour is a foul lie. We get as good weather as anywhere else—certainly as good as London.'

'But different from up here, of course,' she said.

'Well, this is like nowhere else, is it? It's got an atmosphere of its own.'

'Yes,' she said, 'it certainly has. Even the people are different. I mean, that Russian sailor I bumped into on Friday —heavens! if I'd known, I'd have been terrified.'

'Would you?' He looked at her curiously. 'Why?'

'Well, they're all spies, aren't they—I mean with these places up here, the early warning things, the monitoring stations——' he was looking at her now, and there was something in his eyes—but he still was not *sure*. She gave a delicious shiver. 'Heavens, it's nice to know I've got you to protect me today. You would, wouldn't you, if we bumped into a Russian submarine or anything?'

'Emma, have you been talking to anybody?' he said slowly.

She widened her eyes. 'Me? Why do you ask?'

They were heading towards a rocky island, and Douglas slowed the motors, concentrating on his task, not speaking for the moment, swinging round, slowing even more, then the engines put-puttered into silence, the boat rocked gently, and he turned to her and said: 'Right, Emma. Give.'

'Give what?' but her lip trembled with a hidden smile and he took hold of her arms and shook her gently.

'Come on. You know, don't you?'

'Yes.' She smiled at him. 'Greg told us on Friday—after I'd stormed into his house and accused him——'

'You didn't?'

'I did too. And *you*——' she shook herself free of his grasp. 'You're just as sneaky as him. I should have refused to come out with you today.'

He grinned boyishly. 'Sorry, honey, but life's like that. We didn't know. Anyway, let's get ashore, then talk. I'm going to show you round this island, then we'll eat. I want to know how you found out about us—it's nice to know you're on our side anyway.' He wore thick wellingtons, the water was shallow, and he lifted Emma ashore and put her down on the dry shingle.

He passed her the basket of food, which they left on the beach while they set off to explore the island. And as they

158

went along, Emma told him of her growing suspicions, the overheard conversation between him and Greg, and the other tiny things that had eventually grown into something too big and frightening to be hidden any longer. Douglas was a fascinated listener, a growing smile on his face at her words, at the logical sensible way she set them out for him.

'You're a marvel, Emma,' he said at last. 'Care for a job up here?'

She smiled—at least she tried to. What a thought, and if only he could have guessed!

'Heavens, no,' she answered lightly. 'I enjoy my work.' They were scrambling up a steep path, and it seemed only natural that Douglas should take her hand. He pulled her up the last few steps and they stood to get their breath back as they looked out to sea. The boat shimmered in the sun, and gulls flew over with sad cries, eyeing the basket of food, waiting for it to be opened, skimming along, patient . . .

'Anyway, the holiday's nearly over,' she told him. 'I came here for a rest, not to be involved in all this political skulduggery. I'll need a rest when I get back, I think.'

But Douglas wasn't listening. He was looking at her all right, but she could tell his thoughts were on something else—on what, she discovered precisely a few seconds later as he bent his head to kiss her. It took her by surprise and she tried to move away, but in vain. She didn't want any further complications.

'Douglas,' she murmured.

'Hmm? Lovely.' He ignored her protest and kissed her again. But it wasn't the right time, the right place—or the right man. And that last fact was too important to be ignored. She pushed herself free and looked at him.

'We came for a walk, remember?' she said, trying to sound severe, not succeeding, for who could be angry with Douglas, with his open face, his boyish good looks?

159

'That's part of the walk,' he said firmly. 'So don't argue about it.'

'Oh! A male chauvinist pig? I *see*,' she nodded.

He laughed. 'Hardly. But it's asking a lot to expect me to behave myself like a little gentleman all day. Tell me, had Judith really got a headache?'

The question took her by surprise. He was watching her as they walked along. She knew it would be silly to lie. 'No,' she shook her head. 'But she felt like having an easy day, writing letters and so on. You don't mind?'

'Me? Of course not. I'm delighted to have you all to myself. Of course——' he added quickly, 'I like her, but you know the old saying about two's company——' he paused and grinned at her.

'Yes, I do, but I ought——'

'No, you oughtn't.' He put a finger to her lips. 'I don't care how many boy-friends, fiancés or husbands you've got tucked away in the smoke, you're here with me now, and that's all that counts, okay?'

She bobbed her head submissively. 'Yes, sir.'

'And if you call me that again you'll see how much of a male chauvinist pig I can be. So watch it,' he finished severely. He took her hand. 'Come on, race you to that rock.' They ended in a breathless laughing huddle by the giant landmark, Douglas having won by a comfortable few yards—but Emma suspected he had slowed down anyway.

He was nice, she knew that now, had done all along. He was everything you could want in a companion for a day's outing, and she wished that Greg would leave her thoughts for a while. But wishing didn't make some things happen, he was there, a constant presence in her mind, a dark disturbing factor that would not go away ... Greg ... just Greg, always.

And Douglas turned to her as they walked along, and

said, almost as if he could see into her mind: 'What do you think of Greg Halcro?'

She had to compose her face before she could answer, lest she give herself away. There, it was done. 'In what way?' she asked.

'Any way you like. You don't—er—get on very well?'

'You could put it like that,' she answered dryly. 'On the other hand you could say that he's the rudest, most arrogant, aggressive man it's ever been my misfortune to meet——'

'Wow! That's enough to be going on with. Sorry I asked.' He really did seem regretful, and Emma had to smile.

'Sorry, Douglas. He just—oh, I can't put it into words! He was all right, just for a while, after I accused him of searching our house, and he told us why, and who he was—just for a while. But I don't think it's in his nature to be nice for long. How do *you* get on with him, anyway?' She did want to know, yet at the same time she didn't. It was very confusing really.

'Greg? What a man! He's a terrific personality—sorry, I know this may sound absurd to you, after what you've just said, but that's how I find him.'

Somehow, and in the strangest possible way, she was not a bit surprised. Douglas went on, his voice filled with enthusiasm, as if, once launched on the subject, it was going to be difficult to get him off: 'He's got a fund of jokes that—well,' he hesitated. 'Well, he can be very funny at times, believe me. He's had us all in stitches in the bar some evenings.' Emma hid a smile. It was as if she already knew all this. 'He speaks about eight languages fluently—he's been all over the world. Terrific personality.'

She didn't want to ask it, but she had to. 'He's not married, of course?'

161

Then Douglas looked at her, and it was difficult to see what lay behind his eyes, but he shook his head. 'No! This is his life. A chap who was here about a year ago knew him before he came here. He hinted that there had been some woman in Greg's life a few years ago—someone who'd jilted him—and it had soured him for good. Whether it's true or not—and the last thing anyone would do is ask him, believe me—one thing is certain. Our Greg is a woman-hater. I was interested to know what you thought of him, but I wasn't surprised at your opinion. He's off the fair sex good and proper, and that's a fact!'

# CHAPTER TEN

EMMA should have known. It explained those hard kisses—almost contemptuous, she realized now; a gesture, not of affection, but of mockery. She felt suddenly cold. Well, at least she knew where she was. It was a strangely blank, lonely feeling to have. She took a deep breath. Now. Enough.

'Well,' she said lightly, 'let's not waste time on that subject, shall we? I can think of far more interesting things to talk about. You, for instance. Tell me about you.' And she convinced herself that that was what she really wanted to know. Douglas was funny as well. He could be very amusing, and was, as he told her about his life in Manchester, his family, the animals that filled his house, his friends. It was very easy to listen, almost to forget the other disturbing factor. She told him then of her life in the other busy city, and by this time, appetites sharpened, they were making their way back to the beach. The wind lifted Emma's hair and blew it round her cheeks, and she sat down on the flat shingle which was more sheltered, brushed the hair away, and gasped:

'I'm starving!'

Douglas looked at her and laughed. 'You're all rosy-cheeked as well,' he said. 'Don't look at me like that, or I shall want to kiss you again.'

Emma opened her eyes wide. 'That was hunger,' she said. 'And if you don't hurry up and open that basket, I won't be responsible for the consequences.'

'All right, all right.' He fumbled with the catches. 'Ah, there now. Tom hasn't let us down.' There were sandwiches, and a large plastic container that looked as if it might hold fruit salad, and a tin of cream, and several cans of beer.

There was no need of conversation while they were eating, no need to force anything. Douglas really was, Emma reflected, a most comfortable person to be with. Under different circumstances she would have enjoyed their day out thoroughly. She was enjoying it anyway, but the shadow of a certain man was between them—only she made sure that Douglas did not know it.

They sat for a while after eating, then went for a swim. Douglas, as if sensing something, but not sure what it was, did not attempt to kiss Emma again. Once, later in the afternoon, he made a lighthearted remark that was to have unforeseen consequences.

'You're in love with someone, aren't you?' he asked, as Emma climbed over a low wall, and he held her hand to help her over.

'Yes,' she answered. But he didn't ask who it was. If he had she would not have told him.

'I've got a girl in Manchester,' he told her. 'Nothing serious—yet. I've known her all my life, and I suppose I've always taken her for granted—you know, like a kid sister. Then, last time I was home, she called round—she's a friend of my sister's. And something hit me. It was like seeing her for the first time. That's all it is at present. She's still just my sister's friend, but——' he shrugged and gave a wry grin. 'Who knows?'

'And you kissed me! Shame on you!'

He laughed. 'Who wouldn't want to do that? There's no harm in a kiss or two, Emma—it's just a gesture of friendship, you know?'

164

She did know. With him that was all it was. But why then had it been so very different with Greg, when he didn't even like her? But no one could answer that question. It was becoming good to be with him. Blow Greg Halcro and his strange ways. She was here, and she was having a jolly good time, and that was all that mattered.

The evening had become cooler when they returned to the house. Judith greeted them brightly and looked blank when Douglas asked her if she was better. Then she laughed. 'Oh yes, thanks,' she answered, 'much better. Did you have a good day out?'

'Lovely,' said Emma. 'You're staying for supper, Douglas?'

'Yes, please.'

It was late when he left them, and Emma walked towards the boat with him. When they reached the downward path he paused and took her arm lightly. 'Here's hoping we both get what we want,' he said, and she knew what he referred to. He gave her a friendly, almost brotherly kiss, said he would see her in a day or so, and went to his boat.

She watched his departure, waved back and stood there for a moment or two looking out to sea. 'I hope you get your girl,' she whispered softly. But as he didn't know who she was in love with, he could not possibly know how impossible his wish was for her. She turned and went back to the house.

They walked to the village on Monday and bought food and visited the two old ladies, who seemed very pleased to see them. Emma wondered if they could possibly imagine who Greg Halcro really was, and what he did for a living. To them he was a bird-watcher, an eccentric—a man who gave them lifts when he was passing. And that was all. Monday, after that visit and the walk back to the house, dragged interminably, even though there was plenty of washing to be done, and a good satisfying breeze to dry the clothes. And Emma didn't see Greg at all. Not once. He might have been away.

Tuesday morning they went out for a walk and visited Mrs. Stevenson. There too the welcome was warm and genuine. Judith remarked as they returned to Craig House that at least they were doing their fair share of calling on people—and feeling the effect in tightening waistbands. Emma had to agree. There were always home-made scones or oatcakes with every cup of tea, and it was difficult to refuse—especially when the air gave you an appetite anyway. But soon it would be over, and life would get back to normal again. Normal? What, she wondered fleetingly, was that? Was it the busy whirl of life in a capital city where no one had time to stop and talk for fear they missed an appointment, where people rarely smiled because strangers surrounded them anyway?

They were passing the empty schoolhouse and that too was sad in a way, and poignant. Just old people on an island that cried out for children to run across the hard springy heather, and paddle in the cool water that was everywhere, never more than a mile or so away. Emma sighed, and Judith heard it and looked at her. 'Oh dear,' she said. 'What's that for?'

'I was just thinking about life in general, and what a funny thing it is,' she answered.

Judith nodded. 'I know. It hits us all at times. Especially when——' and she stopped.

'When what?'

Judith gave a wry smile. 'When you're in love for the first time,' she said.

Emma closed her eyes. 'We're going home in a few days,' she said. 'I won't see him again.'

Something else happened on Tuesday afternoon that was significant, but Emma was unaware of it. It had begun to rain immediately after lunch, hard driving forceful rain that made you feel glad to be indoors looking out, happy to be inside a warm room, yet hoping all the animals would find shelter ... And they saw Greg's Land-Rover coming from the direction of the village, a blurry image through rain-covered glass. It was Emma who was standing there, and her heart gave a leap, then steadied as she fought for control. It didn't matter. It mustn't matter.

But it did, because he stopped outside their front door instead of passing as he should have, and she saw him get out and dive into the porch. Then came the knock.

She was smiling when she opened the door. No little effort, but she managed it.

'Do come in,' she said.

'Thanks,' he looked briefly at her, his hair dripping, the rain soaking into the shoulders and arms of the grey anorak he wore. Standing in front of her in the living room he was that giant of a man she so well remembered. Judith came in from the kitchen, her hands floury.

'I thought I hadn't imagined voices,' she said. 'Hello, Greg.'

A quick look at Emma. 'The kettle's on for tea. You'll have a cup?'

He seemed hesitant, then: 'Just a cup, thanks.' He fished in an inner pocket and brought out two envelopes which he handed to Emma. 'This is why I've called,' he said. 'I was at the store and Mr. Grant asked me if I'd deliver the mail for you as he wasn't sure when you'd be in again.'

The writing on the top envelope was distinctive. Robert's. She didn't even look at the second one. She put them down on the sideboard, casually. 'Thank you very much,' she said. Judith turned quickly and went into the kitchen again. The significant moment passed.

Emma was terribly aware of Greg, overwhelmingly and powerfully aware of him, and the sensation was stifling her. Quickly, without thought, she said: 'Take off your coat while you drink. I can put it on the fireguard for a minute.'

He took it off, shrugging it away from him casually, handing it to her, revealing the off-white sweater that made him seem broader-shouldered than ever. 'A good idea. Thanks,' he said. 'This is the sort of weather that makes you appreciate a roof overhead, and a good fire.' He glanced at the hearth. 'No more soot trouble?' he enquired.

It was quite odd really. Emma had the feeling that he could sense the indefinable tension as much as she herself could. It sparked in the air like a live electric current surrounding them, filling the room, making her so intensely aware of him that it was almost frightening. If he touched her ... She moved away, holding the coat, spreading it over the fireguard, moving it away from the hearth so that even if it fell it would not get burnt. And hurry up, Judith, she prayed.

'Sit down,' she said. 'Please.'

'Yes.' He took a chair by the window.

'Douglas and I went out on Sunday,' she said, regretting it immediately, but unable to bear any kind of thinking silence with him.

'I know,' he said. 'He told me.' He took out cigarettes. 'Mind if I smoke?' he asked.

'Of course not——' and then Judith came in, and Emma took a deep breath. Thank God. When Judith was there it was not so painful.

'Here we are. You look soaked, Greg. How long will this last, do you think?'

'Thanks.' He took the beaker from her. 'I don't know.

Hours, maybe. Why? Do you have to go anywhere?' Was he going to offer them a lift? thought Emma fleetingly.

'Heavens, no,' Judith smiled. 'I just wondered. It's a real downpour, isn't it?'

'A *doon tüm*, yes.'

'What?'

He grinned at Judith. '*Doon tüm*—Shetland words for a downpour.'

'How lovely.' She repeated the words carefully, tasting them. 'Are you an expert on local expressions?' Emma sat quietly in a corner by the fire—by his coat—and listened. The tension had evaporated, and she was being ignored—which entirely suited her. And she didn't even think about the letter on the sideboard.

He laughed. He had a pleasant laugh, even if you didn't like him—which was ridiculous, for how could you dislike someone you loved? Emma thought she knew. 'Only a few,' he said. 'Quite colourful, some of them are. *Himst*, for instance.'

'What does that mean?'

'Silly or fey. Try it, it's got an evocative sound to it.'

And Emma repeated it to herself, but silently. I am *himst*, she thought, and he has made me so. She half listened to them both talking, and watched Greg when she was sure she was unobserved. So some woman had hurt him badly in the past, had she? How could anyone—no, she told herself firmly, stop that train of thought. It's nothing to do with me. But it was. Oh, it was very much. Because she had suddenly experienced a very primitive surge of dislike for this unknown, shadowy woman from his past, and it was mixed up with jealousy—because he must have loved her very much ... She couldn't hear it any more.

'Excuse me a minute,' she said, and stood up to go out to

the kitchen, leaving them laughing as Judith was repeating very slowly:

'A *peerie grice*—oh, I like that! But we haven't seen *any* little pigs while we've been here, only little horses.'

He was laughing too in response, but the sound was cut off as Emma shut the door behind her and stayed leaning against it for a moment before moving away. She was trembling. There were some pots to be washed, and Judith had been in the middle of making a minced beef and onion pie for their evening meal, and there were scraps of pastry on the table, and flour. How nice it would be to invite him for dinner, she thought. How nice to sit, the three of them at the table, and talk. She put her hand to her head to stop the sudden pain. Was this how love was—painful and an aching inside you all the time?

Oh, the hell with it, she thought. Grow up. Ask him to stay for dinner—he can only say no. And she went straight back into the living room. He was standing up, had just put his beaker in the hearth and was about to pick up his coat from its airing place on the fireguard.

'Would you like to have dinner with us, Greg?' she asked, well aware of Judith's suddenly concealed astonishment.

He looked across the room at Emma. For a moment she thought she saw something—but then it was gone. It had only been a glimpse, a swift fleeting expression in his eyes.

'How nice of you to ask,' he said. 'But I'm afraid I must refuse. I'm very—busy—tonight.'

It was like a blow to the face. Emma smiled. 'That's quite all right,' she said. 'It was just a thought.'

Yet the next few minutes of his departure were a hazy blur to her. She took nothing in, she stood there, and there was within her a feeling quite new to her—humiliation. She should never have asked. Never.

170

Judith closed the door after him and looked across the room at her friend. There was that in her eyes that made Emma say quickly: 'It's all right, really. I knew he wouldn't. It was just a silly impulse.'

'Of course,' Judith answered gently. She looked at the sideboard. 'Two letters, I wonder if one of them's for me.' She went over to pick them up and Emma watched her.

'One isn't,' she said. 'Because it's from Robert.'

'Hmm, both yours. Aren't you going to open them?'

Emma took the second one, putting the one with that distinctive black writing down again. She opened the type-written letter, and read it, then passed it to Judith. 'Here,' she said dully. 'What do you think of that?'

Judith read it, then again more slowly, and looked up, eyes shining.

'Why, Emma,' she said, 'that's marvellous!'

'Yes, isn't it?' She took the letter back and glanced at it again. How strange that this letter only weeks before would have sent her round the room crying whoopee. Because the chance of a three-week yacht trip, all expenses paid, with the odd spot of modelling on the Greek Islands for a highly reputable magazine, was every model's dream. It had been Emma's too. Not now.

'You'll phone, of course?' Judith asked anxiously.

'Yes, I'll phone.' It was only good manners to let her agent know immediately. She looked out of the window. The rain lashed down ceaselessly, with no signs of stopping, and it was nearly three o'clock.

'I'd better go now,' she said. 'You stay here, Judith—and have a nice hot cuppa waiting for me when I get back.'

'But I——'

'No buts,' Emma said firmly. 'You're in no condition. Besides, I can run——'

'Do you think Greg——'

171

'*No!*'

Judith shrugged. 'All right,' she said. 'All right. But aren't you going to read Robert's letter before you go?'

She had forgotten about it! She had *forgotten*. Emma picked it up again. 'No, I'm not going to read it at all.' And she knelt by the fire and pushed it into the yellow crackling flames. Tears filled her eyes so that everything melted into a blur.

'Oh, Emma!' She heard Judith's soft anguished cry, but she was turning now, leaving it, going into the kitchen for her mac and a pair of wellingtons.

As she opened the front door, Judith said: 'Money— have you got plenty of tens?'

'No!' She gave a wry smile. Perhaps the walk in the pouring rain—what was it? A *doon tüm*?—would do her good. She needed something to clear her head.

A few minutes later, with her pocket full of coins, Emma set off down the slithery path to the road. She didn't look back once. And on the main road she began to run. The rain was all about her, a shimmery silver grey wall of sound, in her eyes and mouth, cleansing her face, one or two drops escaping down inside her collar, cool, strangely refreshing.

The long horn blast didn't register at first, but she turned instinctively round and stopped because the Land-Rover was nearly on her—would he have run her over? She would not have been surprised.

'Get in.'

She looked, but only for a moment. The next second she was scrambling in, and the engine rumbled into life, and Greg Halcro said: 'Where are you going? To phone?'

'Yes.' She wiped her face with a handkerchief from her pocket and put it back. The windscreen wipers whirred busily back and forth, seemingly having no effect on that driving rain.

'Why didn't you ask me for a lift?' he asked, and she turned to him in astonishment. Could she have heard him correctly?

'What?'

'I said—why didn't you ask?'

'Ask *you*!' It came out not quite as she intended, but it would do.

He gave her a level glance, then turned to concentrate on his driving. 'All right,' Emma said. 'I'm sorry. I didn't mean it quite like that. It's very good of you to stop for me. I would have been soaked by now.'

'Yes, you would.' And he drove on in silence. I've done it again, she thought miserably. Why bother trying? We're miles apart in every way. She turned slightly away to look out of the side window, but all she could see was the faint blurry image of the sea running constantly beside them, going on for ever . . .

'I'll call at the old ladies' while you phone, then I'll run you back.'

For a moment she didn't realize the exact significance of his words. Then she did. She swallowed hard and asked, in quite a small voice: 'Do you mean you only came out f-for me?'

'Right in one.' Nothing in his voice—yet was there perhaps something?

'Oh!'

'Well, that's a change,' he added dryly. 'To see you lost for words, I mean.'

He didn't need to explain—she had already know what he meant.

'What can I say?'

'Nothing. Nothing at all,' he answered. 'We're nearly there, okay?'

'Yes. Thank you.' She got out and ran to the phone box.

173

Inside she saw her face in the mirror. Greg Halcro had the continued ability to surprise her.

Her agent was busy, as always. She tried hard to project enthusiasm into her voice as she thanked him for the letter and the offer and told him she would be back in London for weekend.

'I'll bet you'll be glad to get back,' his voice crackled over the wires from that infinity away. 'For heaven's sake, what is there to *do* up there?'

She couldn't even begin to tell him. She was watching the Land-Rover parked outside the little house with a red door. Waiting for her.

'Yes, it'll be good to get into the swing of things again,' she told him. 'Thanks again, Lennie. I'll be in touch at weekend.'

She put the telephone down slowly. Silence, save for the drumming rain. She went out of the box and ran towards that bright red front door. A welcoming place, and the man she loved inside.

He was drinking tea, and the cat stretched out luxuriously on the hearthrug had winked at her and for a moment she thought that this would be how it was if they were married.

'I'll away and get you a cup,' shouted the elder sister, and vanished into the kitchen, and for a moment she and Greg were alone in the room. Their eyes met.

'Make your call all right?' he asked. It broke the spell. Because just for a second there had been no tension, no enmity, there had been just the two of them, and almost a touch of magic...

Her imagination, of course. 'Yes, thanks,' she answered.

'Good. We'll set off back soon—better drink some tea first, or they'll be hurt.'

'Yes, of course.'

174

Then the two women were with them, scones were being produced, and it was all nice and normal again. She tried hard, she really did, but it was difficult to concentrate on the conversation, because he was there. He was like a different man with them. He made them laugh, their eyes sparkled with animation as they spoke, these two dear old ladies who didn't get enough visitors, and who always made you so very welcome. She could watch him without his knowing, because she was to the side, slightly behind him, and he was in profile. He had strong features—she already knew that, his face was imprinted indelibly on her mind for ever, and it was pleasant torture to watch him, to see the changing expressions, even a kind of warmth, as he spoke. Then he looked at his watch—she would have sworn regretfully—and said: 'I hate to have to go, but I have work to do, and I know Emma is busy.'

'Yes,' she smiled at their hostesses. 'But it's been lovely to see you.'

'You must call any time—remember, any time,' was the shouted farewell from the door as they ran quickly to the parked vehicle. But I won't be here, Emma thought as she scrambled in.

There was silence for several minutes after they started up along the road. It was Emma who broke it. 'They like you,' she said.

'Yes, I do have a certain effect on women,' was the flippant reply. She took a deep breath. Don't start, she told herself. Ignore it. He glanced at her.

'Lost it again?'

'Are you trying to get me mad?'

'Not at all. What makes you think that?'

'Everything you say, if you want to know.'

'I know your trouble—you have no sense of humour.'

She wasn't going to let him get away with that. 'Listen,'

she said. 'There's absolutely nothing wrong with my sense of humour, thank you. I've had a lot to put up with since coming to your little island, one way or another, and I don't need to go over the details, I'm quite sure. I just don't intend to argue with you any more, that's all. It's not——' she faltered slightly, 'worth it.'

'Ah!' It was a long-drawn-out, sympathetic 'ah', but it was mocking too. Emma bit her lip hard. Never had there been a man who could so infuriate her.

She turned and looked out of the window, breathing very steadily and calmly. And Greg added: 'Never mind, it's not for much longer, is it? And he'll be glad to see you.'

'He?' She didn't know who he meant. 'Who?'

'The boy-friend. The one you just phoned.'

She was about to correct him, but stopped herself in time. So that was what he imagined. What did it matter anyway? It was almost funny, but just for a few moments she wondered if she had indeed lost her sense of humour, because not for anything could she have laughed.

'I dare say,' she said quietly. If only he knew the truth!

He did not speak again, and they drove in silence to Craig House. As Emma got out she thanked him, said goodbye and ran in.

And then it was Wednesday, and they had decided to leave on Friday morning. Time suddenly seemed to be flying past all too quickly. On Thursday, Emma decided, she would phone Dougall and ask if he would pick them up and take them back to Lerwick. Listening to the radio after breakfasting that Wednesday morning, she thought over all that had happened. No one would believe it, she knew, and she didn't want to tell anyone either. She had completely forgotten Robert's letter, unread and burnt.

She was washing up the pots while Judith made the beds

176

upstairs, looking out of the window at the sunshine outside, wondering how they would pass the day. Would Douglas call? It would be nice to see him. She had slept badly, dreaming strange sad dreams of waiting on railway stations for a train that never came, of wandering along empty platforms wondering where everyone had gone, unable to talk to anyone anyway because tears choked her. She had woken up and her pillow was wet with them.

She made a determined effort to appear her normal self, and by the time Judith came down, had succeeded.

'How about some sunbathing on the beach?' she suggested to her friend.

Judith's eyebrows shot up.

'Do you think it's warm enough?' she asked doubtfully.

'It will be in a certain spot on the beach. I'll show you. We can give it a try, and if we get goose pimples, we can always change and go and have a good look over the castle. Okay?'

'Okay,' Judith agreed. 'It certainly seems warm enough, looking out.'

Half an hour later they were in swimsuits and stretched out on rugs on the sand. Sheltered from any wind by craggy rocks, the sun beat down on them without interruption, and Emma closed her eyes trying to visualize herself on a yacht doing just this, with the same sun on her then. It will be the best thing, she thought. It will help me to forget . . .

There was a voice calling her name, only it wasn't Greg's and it wasn't Douglas's. It was . . . It couldn't be! Emma sat up suddenly—and so did Judith.

'Did you hear it?'

Judith nodded. 'Yes. It sounded like—like Robert.'

'Oh no, oh no!' Emma scrambled to her feet, and shading her eyes, looked towards the cliff to see Robert standing there. She closed her eyes. He was still there when she opened them.

He came down slowly, carefully, and he was looking at her.

'Emma,' he said. 'I've come a long way.'

'I—how did you know where we were?' she asked, because it was all she could think of to say. Good-looking in his own dark way, he seemed faintly unsure of himself as he reached her and stood before her.

'Your neighbour told me,' he answered. 'Emma, I want to talk to you.'

Judith came up. 'Hello, Robert,' she said. 'Look, if you two want to talk, I'll go back to the house.'

'No—wait,' Emma began, but Robert cut in:

'Yes, please, if you don't mind, Judith.'

'I don't mind.' She looked at Emma. 'Put your rug over you, you'll catch cold.'

'Yes, I will.' Robert picked it up and put the plaid travelling rug over Emma's shoulders as Judith began climbing up the path. Emma was beginning to shiver, but it was not with cold.

'Didn't you get my letter?' she asked him, when Judith had gone.

'Why do you think I'm here?' Had she ever imagined herself to be in love with him? Emma felt faintly surprised. His light blue eyes held anger, but it didn't move her as it would once have done. She didn't *care*.

'And you've come all this way?'

'Yes. Don't tell me you didn't get *my* letter?'

She took a deep breath. 'I burnt it. Robert, listen——'

'No, *you* listen. Something's happened to you while you've been here, I can see it. What—or should I say who, is it?'

'No. It's nothing. But we've finished—I told you——'

'No, we haven't. That row—everyone has them—it

178

didn't mean——'

'But it did. For me it did.' She tried to move away, but he caught her arm.

'I don't believe you. You don't just stop loving someone like that.'

'You're hurting my arm, Robert. I'm sorry—if I'd known you were coming I'd have prevented you. Don't you see? I thought I loved you, but I don't. That row—if it hadn't been that it would have been something else. Can't you accept that?'

'No.' He took his hand away from her arm. 'I don't accept anything. We're not finished, and I'll prove it to you. It's this place—what a God-forsaken hole to get to—why the hell you wanted to come here I'll never know—but let me get you away from here and you'll see. Things will get back to normal again.'

That was what everyone seemed to be trying to tell her. It was like some sort of conspiracy to get her off Skeila. How comical! She began to laugh, then turned and ran towards the path to get away from Robert. He ran after her and caught her as she was about to start up the path, and she stumbled on the loose shingle and he held her to him.

'Listen,' he said. 'You mustn't run away from me. Not from me.'

'Yes.' She was breathless now. She didn't want him to try and kiss her, not at all. 'Robert, let's go back to the house and talk.'

'With Judith there?'

'She'll go in another room. I'm getting cold here. Please.'

She had not yet got over the shock of his arrival. She should have read his letter instead of burning it, although it might have been too late, even then. He could have already set off when his letter reached Craig House. She knew she should feel flattered because he had travelled so many hundreds of miles to be with her—but she didn't. There was a disturbing blankness inside her, and she tried to prevent it showing, because she also had no desire to hurt him.

'All right, if that's what you want, Emma.'

It's not what I want, she thought, because I wish you weren't here, but I can't tell you that. They walked upwards, across springy turf, newly rain-washed and greener, but she knew that to him it meant nothing. He would see no beauty here, none of the sheer rugged splendour that could take your breath away. To him, Skeila was just a 'God-forsaken hole,' and that was all.

Judith was changed when they went in, and had the kettle on for tea. She came in from the kitchen. 'Are you hungry, Robert?' she asked him. 'We'll be having lunch in about an hour, but if you'd like something first——'

'That will do fine, thanks. I'm not hungry at all.' He was clearly impatient to talk, and while Emma had no wish to do so, it was useless to delay the inevitable, she knew. The sooner the air was cleared, the better for everybody. Yet it would not be easy, she knew that too.

'I'll go and get into something warmer,' she said. 'I won't be a minute.'

Judith followed her upstairs. 'You want to talk. Shall I go out?' she asked.

Emma, busily stripping off her swimsuit, pulled a face. 'It's no good putting it off,' she answered. 'But don't go out on my account, please——'

'I'll stay up here and read. Don't forget to switch off the kettle. Go on, love,' she patted Emma's arm. 'Do what's right.'

'I'll try. Thanks, Judith.' She pulled on slim-fitting brown check trews and eased a white sweater over her head. Then, leaving Judith, she ran down to join Robert.

She realized quite soon that he wasn't prepared to be-lieve her reasons for the end of their engagement. Pacing up and down the sitting room, he turned violently and cut in on what she was saying.

'For heaven's sake, Emma, I didn't come all this way to hear these feeble reasons from you. What do you think I am? I need you—I love you, dammit.'

'You may need me, but you don't love me.' It was strange how calm she had suddenly become. She looked at him, and he stood quite still. 'I realize that now, Robert. It's your pride—your vanity if you like—that brought you up here. You've never been turned down before by any wo-man, have you?' She was remembering so many things that hadn't seemed to matter during the brief term of their en-gagement. 'I'm sorry, but there it is.'

He had gone almost white. She noticed that too, and it disturbed her, but only because she felt sorry for him. She had never thought she would feel pity for Robert. He moved towards her and quite suddenly tried to take her in his arms. 'No, Robert, please——' her protests went un-heeded as he took hold of her forcefully and began to kiss her. She struggled, but vainly. He was far too strong. Noth-ing would make her respond, and after a few moments he released her, his eyes dark with anger.

'Thanks,' he grated.

'I didn't ask——'

'Who is it? That one——' he jerked his head savagely in the direction of Greg's house—'next door?'

'What on earth——' she began, frightened.

'Come on, I know you that well at least—though not as well as I thought, apparently. Has he been sweet-talking you? Giving you a line?'

She shrugged his hands away. 'Don't be stupid.' But something must have betrayed her, something in her eyes, because he took hold of her again swiftly.

'Yes, I can see it written on your face. My God! I bet he thought it was his birthday when you arrived. I'll bet he's been having——'

She hit him then. She didn't know what he had been about to say, but she could imagine, and she didn't want to hear it.

For an explosive moment he faced her, then turned and wrenched the front door open. 'Wait, Robert—where are you going?' She tried to stop him, but he flung her restraining arm from him and went out. Catching her breath, Emma ran after him.

She reached him as he got to Greg's door and banged it hard. 'For God's sake, Robert,' she gasped, 'please come back. I'll tell you——'

Too late. The door opened, and Greg stood there. Greg, tall, dark, unsmiling. 'Yes?' he said, and Robert pushed forward and answered:

'I want to talk to *you*.'

'Do you now?'

'It's all right, Greg,' Emma spoke frantically. This was like a nightmare. Everything—everyone was going mad.

'Is it? You'd better come in,' and he held the door open.

'No,' said Robert. 'Just you and me.' He turned to Emma. 'Not you.'

'Yes—I——'

'Perhaps Emma can decide for herself,' said Greg. She had never seen him quite like that before. Intimidating in a way. He looked at her. 'Well?'

'Yes. I want to——' But she didn't really. At the same time she wanted to stop Robert saying the things—the awful things she knew he would say. And Robert turned on her.

'You've done enough,' he said tautly. 'Go back *now*——'

and he put out his arms to push her, and Greg said:

'I wouldn't touch her if I were you.'

It was as if Robert exploded then. He whirled back on Greg, shouted:

'Shut up, you——' and swung a fist straight towards the other's face.

Emma was sobbing. Her only thought was for Greg, that he might be hurt. This ghastly nightmare was too awful to bear. She jumped forward without thinking, was knocked violently to one side by a flailing arm—Robert's—and went staggering back, dazed.

She saw the punch, but it never landed because Greg turned sideways, and Robert was carried forward by his own momentum. There was a crack, a thud, the sound of a man's voice cursing fluently, and she put her hand to her mouth, feeling sick. Violence, two men fighting like animals —and it was all her doing. All hers. She should never have come. Never, never . . .

Trembling, still shaken with the force of the push that had sent her staggering, Emma, overwhelmed with horror, turned and ran. Anywhere to get away, anywhere at all.

She ran fleetly, instinct guiding her safely over rough ground, avoiding the treacherous holes that could trip and injure her. She ran on heedless of everything, and there was a wild music filling her ears, and her breath was ragged and short because she could not stop now, and her tears and sobs mingled with the wind on her face, burning her, making her hot and dizzy.

She stumbled at last, and fell, and she was by a wall which provided shelter, so she crawled near to it and put her head in her hands, cradling herself into as small a shape as possible because there was nowhere to hide. Nowhere to hide from herself.

Gradually her breathing returned to normal, but she still

remained there. She would have to leave soon, but not yet, not just yet. There was a time to stop running away, a time to face the things which had to be faced, and that time was now. She owed it to herself, to Judith, to Robert—and to Greg.

Slowly, shakily, Emma stood up, heard a man's voice call her, and saw Greg coming towards her. Greg. Her lips formed the name, but silently. And she waited, because just at that moment, she could not move.

He reached her, and she waited for the anger, the scorn. She was ready for him, and tilted her chin up in a last gesture of defiance.

And Greg said softly: 'Oh, Emma, Emma. Why did you run away?'

It was not what she had expected. She looked blankly at him, utterly bewildered, and he reached out to touch her arm, very gently.

'Why do you tremble so?' he asked.

'Am I? I don't—know.' But she did. She was frightened.

'Judith told me,' he said. 'I guessed something when your —your friend came swinging punches, but it took Judith to tell me in so many words.'

'Judith?' she repeated idiotically. 'What did she s-say?'

'The truth. What else?'

She shook her head. 'Oh no—oh no!'

'Oh yes. Come on back, love. Your—I mean Robert is waiting and nursing a sore jaw. I don't fancy leaving him too long with her. Come on, Emma.' He put his arm round her, and it was just right.

But she could not go back yet. There was something to be explained first, a confession to be made because lies would not do. 'Wait, Greg,' she said. 'I must tell you first— why Robert wanted to hurt you. He guessed that I——' she faltered. It was a hundred times more difficult than she had anticipated.

'That you love me?' Greg was grinning at her, a Cheshire cat grin, an expression not of scorn or derision but of rightness. 'Thank God for Robert, that's all I can say. If it took him to realize——'

'You're not laughing?' She really must be going crazy.

'I'm not laughing because there's nothing to laugh at. Don't you *know*?'

'Know what?' They were walking back to the houses, now in sight, not so far away at all.

'Know why I've been such an aggressive swine—like a bear with a sore head—like an arrogant devil with you. Because I'd fallen hard—and I fought it like hell. Right up until five minutes ago, when I socked the man I thought you loved—and then knew the truth about myself.'

'Oh!'

He squeezed her to him. 'Is that all you can say?'

'For a moment, yes. You thought—ah!' It was becoming clearer every minute.

'Yes, I did. More fool me. I think there's a lot of explaining to do, on both sides, but first things first. I'm going to put through a call to Douglas. I'm sure Robert would appreciate a lift back to Lerwick just as soon as possible. *Then* we can talk.'

'Robert. Oh, poor Robert.' She couldn't help it.

Greg gave her one of his level grey glances. 'He'll get over it. He's not staying here, and that's that. Come on, love. We can at least give the poor devil some food before we send him winging back to London. I left the dogs sitting in front of him and told him he'd be advised not to make any sudden moves.' He laughed. 'I ought to thank him really, for letting me find you—for letting me see.' He stopped. 'Just time for a kiss, I think.' And he proceeded to demonstrate very nicely.

And then they walked back to Craig House hand in hand, Emma and her dark Viking, and the future stretched before them like the sea, endlessly.

# OMNIBUS — The 3 in 1 HARLEQUIN
only $1.75 per volume

Here is a great new exciting idea from Harlequin.
THREE GREAT ROMANCES — complete and
unabridged — BY THE SAME AUTHOR — in one
deluxe paperback volume — for the unbelievably
low price of only $1.75 per volume.

We have chosen some of the finest works of four
world-famous authors . . .

SARA SEALE

JANE ARBOR

ANNE WEALE

ESSIE SUMMERS ②

. . . and reprinted them in the 3 in 1 Omnibus.
Almost 600 pages of pure entertainment for just
$1.75 each. A TRULY "JUMBO" READ!

These four Harlequin Omnibus volumes are now
available. The following pages list the exciting
novels by each author.

Climb aboard the Harlequin Omnibus now! The
coupon below is provided for your convenience in
ordering.

# Sara Seale

## Omnibus

Her natural talent for creating the very finest in romantic fiction has been acknowledged and enjoyed by a great many readers since very early in Miss Seale's career. Here, we have chosen three perfect examples of her best loved and most cherished stories.

. . . . . . . . . . CONTAINING:

QUEEN OF HEARTS . . . when Selina presented herself to her new employer at Barn Close, the exclusive country hotel in Coney Combe, Devonshire, Max Savant had one thought, to send this "child" on her way. Now, it was impossible for him to imagine himself, or his hotel being without her. But, he must, for he has just become engaged to Val Proctor . . . (#1324).

PENNY PLAIN . . . at Plovers Farm, near the village of Chode, in England, Miss Emma Clay is employed as assistant and companion to the rather spoilt young lady, Mariam Mills. Their relationship proves to be rather stormy, not the least cause of which is the country vet, in his country tweeds, the uncompromising Max Grainger . . . (#1197).

GREEN GIRL . . . Harriet listened to the incredible suggestion that she marry this total stranger and thus solve her dilemma, and the trouble which he himself was in. Whilst she knew full well that her own plight was quite hopeless, instinct warned her that Duff Lonnegan's trouble was far more serious than even he knew . . . (#1045).

$1.75 per volume

# Jane Arbor
## Omnibus

Jane Arbor chooses inspiring locations, peopled with the most life-like characters, — then inter weaves her gripping narratives. Her achievements have brought her world renown as a distinguished author of romantic fiction.

. . . . . . . . . . CONTAINING:

A GIRL NAMED SMITH . . . Mary Smith, a most uninspiring name, a mouselike personality and a decidedly unglamorous appearance. That was how Mary saw herself. If this description had fitted, it would have been a great pleasure to the scheming Leonie Crispin, and could have avoided a great deal of misunderstanding between Mary, Leonie and the handsomely attractive Clive Derwent . . . (#1000).

KINGFISHER TIDE . . . Rose Drake was about to realize her most cherished dream — to return to the small village of Maurinaire, France. To manage her aunt's boutique shop produced grand illusions for Rose, but from the very day of her arrival, they were turned to dismay. The man responsible was the town's chief landowner and seigneur, a tyrant — living back in the days of feudalism . . . (#950).

THE CYPRESS GARDEN . . . at the Villa Fontana in the Albano Hills in Italy, the young, pretty Alessandra Rhode is subjected to a cruel deception which creates enormous complications in her life. The two handsome brothers who participate come to pay dearly for their deceit — particularly, the one who falls in love . . . (#1336).

$1.75 per volume

# Anne Weale

## Omnibus

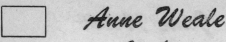

The magic which is produced from the pen of this famous writer is quite unique. Her style of narrative and the authenticity of her stories afford her readers unlimited pleasure in each of her very fine novels.

. . . . . . . . . . CONTAINING:

THE SEA WAIF . . . it couldn't be, could it? Sara Winchester the beautiful and talented singer stood motionless gazing at the painting in the gallery window. As she tried to focus through her tears, her thoughts went racing back to her sixteenth birthday, almost six years ago, and the first time she set eyes on the sleek black-hulled sloop "Sea Wolf", and its owner, Jonathon "Joe" Logan . . . (#1123).

THE FEAST OF SARA . . . as Joceline read and re-read the almost desperate letter just received from cousin Camilla in France, pleading with Joceline to come and be with her, she sensed that something was terribly wrong. Immediately, she prepares to leave for France, filled with misgivings; afraid of learning the reason for her cousin's frantic plea . . . (#1007).

DOCTOR IN MALAYA . . . Andrea Fleming desperately wanted to accompany the film crew on the expedition, but Doctor James Ferguson adamantly refused stating that if she went along, he would refuse to guide them. But, Guy Ramsey had other ideas, and cunningly devised a scheme whereby Andrea would join them — in a manner which the Doctor could not oppose . . . (#914).

$1.75 per volume

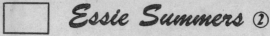

# Essie Summers ②

## Omnibus

Without doubt, Miss Summers has become the first lady among those who write of the joy and splendour of romance. Her frequent use of locations in New Zealand, the country of her birth, has a timeless appeal to her readers throughout the world.

. . . . . . . . . . . CONTAINING:

HIS SERENE MISS SMITH . . . she was very certain that never again, under any circumstances would she ever become involved with a member of the male management of any firm where she was employed. Then, William Durbridge came thundering into her life, and before long, was making his way straight to her heart . . . (#1093).

THE MASTER OF TAWHAI . . . Tawhai Hills Estate lay deep in the green rolling country of South Canterbury, New Zealand. It was here that the wealthy young Rowena Fotheringham came to work in the hope of being accepted for herself — not her fortune. She could easily have been, had she not decided to deceive the very first man who had ever really cared for her, complicating both their lives . . . (#910).

A PLACE CALLED PARADISE . . . no one must ever know the truth, the reason why Annabel Lee had come to Paradise, an isolated plateau at the head of Lake Wakatipu in New Zealand. She did not know how deeply she would come to love a man called Gideon Darroch, nor how it would affect him — if he learned her secret . . . (#1156).

$1.75 per volume